"I'm sorry I just h[...]
there this morning[...]

"You were there to keep us safe. You didn't owe us anything else. We appreciate it."

So formal, he thought. "That's not all it was, and you know it. Don't you?"

The pained look in her eyes showed her reluctance to have this conversation. But ignoring the attraction between them hadn't seemed to work very well so far. Maybe getting it out in the open and putting it to rest was the only solution.

"What do you want from me?"

"I'm not a good bet for happily ever after. Been there, done that, got burned."

Her lips curved slightly. "Same here."

"But that doesn't mean I'm not still a grown man."

"With grown man needs?"

He nodded.

"Is this some sort of proposition?"

"I'm sorry I just hot-footed it out of there this morning. That was rude."

PAULA GRAVES

MAJOR NANNY

TORONTO NEW YORK LONDON
AMSTERDAM PARIS SYDNEY HAMBURG
STOCKHOLM ATHENS TOKYO MILAN MADRID
PRAGUE WARSAW BUDAPEST AUCKLAND

For my editor, Allison, who trusted me enough to ask me to take on
this project. And for my fellow Daddy Corps authors, who helped
make this experience so much fun.

Special thanks and acknowledgment to Paula Graves for her
contribution to the Daddy Corps series.

ISBN-13: 978-0-373-69572-0

MAJOR NANNY

Copyright © 2011 by Harlequin Books S.A.

ABOUT THE AUTHOR

Alabama native Paula Graves wrote her first book, a mystery starring herself and her neighborhood friends, at the age of six. A voracious reader, Paula loves books that pair tantalizing mystery with compelling romance. When she's not reading or writing, she works as a creative director for a Birmingham advertising agency and spends time with her family and friends. She is a member of Southern Magic Romance Writers, Heart of Dixie Romance Writers and Romance Writers of America.

Paula invites readers to visit her website, www.paulagraves.com.

Books by Paula Graves

CAST OF CHARACTERS

Stacy Giordano—A single mom to a child with Asperger's syndrome as well as the Texas governor's aide-de-camp, the last thing Stacy needs to deal with is another threat to the governor's life—especially when it puts her and her young son in the line of fire.

Harlan McClain—The governor taps the Corps Security and Investigations agent to head security for an upcoming fundraiser—and work side by side with Stacy. Can he keep the governor and her pretty aide safe from a ruthless assassin?

Zachary Giordano—Stacy's young son is struggling to fit into a world that makes no sense to him. But does he have a vital clue to the mystery of who's stalking his mother locked in his mind?

Lila Lockhart—The Texas governor's announced intention to run for president was greeted by a deadly bomb blast. Is she crazy to hold another fundraiser within a couple of weeks of the assassination attempt?

Bart Bellows—Lila's dear friend owns Corps Security and Investigations. Did he make a mistake assigning Harlan McClain to the governor's security staff?

Greg Merritt—Governor Lockhart's new campaign manager is a political shark. Can Stacy trust him to have the governor's best interests at heart?

Trevor Lewis—The young stable groom has taken a liking to Stacy and her young son, Zachary. But what are his true motives for befriending them?

Jeff Appleton—The Freedom, Texas, deputy is leading the investigation into some very personal threats against Stacy. But is he looking in the wrong direction?

Planet Justice—The anarchistic antiglobalization group is determined to hold a peaceful protest outside the governor's fundraiser. But are there elements within the group whose intentions are anything but peaceful?

Chapter One

The bomb went off, and for a minute, Harlan McClain was back on a dusty road in Iraq, his ears ringing. Everything around him moved in slow motion—debris flying, people falling.

There were screams. Always screams. The training never prevented the screaming.

You're not in Iraq. You're in Austin, Texas, and a bomb just went off. Get your backside in gear.

Over a decade of Marine Corps training taking over as chaos unfolded around him, he scanned the area for a quick damage assessment. Car bomb. Not a huge one—the blast radius wasn't anywhere near the size of something like Oklahoma City—but the dais where Governor Lila Lockhart had stood moments earlier was a ruin, reduced to jagged metal and splintered wood.

Was the governor buried somewhere under the debris?

The crowd surrounding the platform had already begun to disperse in panic, leaving behind some of the fallen. Many were still moving, trying to drag themselves to safety. Others lay motionless in the grass in front of the dais.

Triage, he thought, pulling out his cell phone to call 911. His call was one of many, he discovered. To his relief, the dispatcher told him units were already responding. But he couldn't sit tight waiting for the cavalry to arrive—some of these people might not survive the wait.

As he hurried toward the first fallen victim, a slim, dark-haired woman raced across his path, heading toward the collapsed platform. Blood stained the side of her face without obscuring her delicate profile. Pretty, he thought. Scared as hell. She looked familiar.

"Governor!" she cried, trying to pull away a piece of metal from the pile.

Harlan raced forward to stop her. The wrong move could bring the rest of the debris falling down on top of anyone buried underneath. And the last time he'd seen his boss, Bart Bellows had been only a few feet from Lila Lockhart.

"Don't try to move anything," he barked, his voice coming out more gruff than he'd intended.

She turned a fierce glare his way. "The governor is under there."

"And if you do the wrong thing, you could bring the rest of this mess crashing in on her."

Her nostrils flared. "You were with Bart."

"Harlan McClain." He nodded, remembering where he'd seen her before. "You're the governor's aide, right?"

"Stacy Giordano." She pressed her fingertips to the side of her head. When she drew them away, they were bloody. Her face went even paler. "What happened? Was it a bomb?"

"Yeah, I'm pretty sure."

She shook her head, looking stunned and scared. "But Frank Dorian is in jail."

He'd had the same thought. Even Bart, who was a suspicious old cuss, had thought that stopping Frank Dorian solved Governor Lockhart's problem. Dorian had come damned close to killing the governor before Wade Coltrane had stopped him, but once he was in custody, everyone at

Corps Security Investigations had thought the trouble was over.

Harlan should have known better. Trouble never went away for long.

"We need to help the injured." He caught her arm, making her gasp. He loosened his grip, tried to soften his voice. She looked shell-shocked and he didn't need to spook her any further. "Go find as many able-bodied people as you can. We need to start some sort of triage—"

She straightened, as if she'd found her core of steel. "Okay." Her chin lifted and her eyes flashed with determination as she headed out in search of help.

He wasn't surprised when she returned a few minutes later with several people in tow. Most had clearly survived the blast themselves, their clothing covered with grime and fine debris. Some, like Stacy, had cuts and scrapes, but they all seemed relieved to have a purpose—something to take their minds off witnessing their world upended.

Sometimes, Harlan knew, finding something useful to do was the only thing that kept you sane in a crazy world.

He sent Stacy Giordano and her army in search of people who were moving around, while he checked on the ones who weren't moving. Unlike his civilian helpers, he had plenty of experience in dealing with mortality. Too much experience.

He found two D.O.A.s and a couple more who might not make it. As he moved to the next body—a man in a state trooper uniform lying near the mangled remains of the dais—he heard sirens approaching at a clip.

"It's Chip!" Stacy Giordano rushed past him toward the state trooper. "He's part of the governor's security detail."

Harlan raced to catch up, not sure what she'd find when she reached the trooper's still body.

Stacy crouched next to the man, her fingers on his carotid. "He's alive," she said briskly. Her hands moved over his body, searching for injuries. She moved with a sureness that caught Harlan by surprise.

"You a nurse or something?"

She glanced at him. "No. Search and rescue medic training. There's a lump here at the back of his head. Skull feels intact, but it may be a concussion." She checked the man's eyes with a small penlight attached to a keychain. "Pupils reactive. Good sign."

The man made a low groaning sound.

"EMTs are arriving. We should back off, let them work," Harlan suggested.

"There aren't going to be enough for everybody. Not yet—"

He caught her arm and tugged her to a standing position. "We'll be in the way. And we don't know that we've seen the last of the blasts."

Her eyes widened. "You think there could be more coming?"

"It's possible," he admitted. "Sometimes there's a secondary device—"

"To hit the first responders." Stacy's jaw squared. "Then we'd better find the governor and get her out of here." She started toward the back of the dais before he could stop her.

He jogged to catch up.

"She was standing back here," Stacy called over her shoulder, "so if she dropped with the dais—"

Harlan spotted a flash of pale blue under the tangle of metal piping and wooden slats that had once constituted the bunting-draped platform where Lila Lockhart had declared her intention to run for higher office. Lila had been wearing a light blue suit, hadn't she?

"Lila!" Stacy dashed forward. "Lila, can you hear me?"

"I'm stuck under this damned mess!" Lila called out, her

voice surprisingly strong. "I must've bumped my head—I was out a few seconds—"

"Hold still—you don't want to cause yourself more injury," Harlan warned. "Did you see what happened to Bart?"

"He was right behind me—"

"I'm over here." A man's voice, weak and strained, came from somewhere behind Harlan.

Harlan turned to see a large chunk of the dais had broken off and flown backward in the blast, landing sideways in a shallow rill in the capitol grounds. "Bart?"

"Knocked me clean on my backside!" Bart called out, his voice a little stronger. "But I can't get my chair up."

"Keep her from moving," Harlan ordered Stacy before he hurried to the second debris site. To his relief, Bart had been thrown clear of the twisted tangle of wood and metal, but the old man and his wheelchair both lay on their sides in the grass beyond the rill.

"I'm afraid this is probably a goner," Harlan said as he picked up the wheelchair, pushing it away from Bart's useless legs to free them. He grimaced as his scarred right hand twinged where he gripped the chair handle.

"Is Lila okay?" Bart asked.

"She's alive. She's trapped under the debris, but she sounds good. The paramedics are on the way."

"Who did this? Frank Dorian's in jail."

"I don't know." Harlan ran his hands over Bart's body, looking for injuries. He didn't feel any obvious broken bones, and the old man seemed bright-eyed and lucid. "Do you have any pain anywhere?"

Bart shook his head. "The explosion flung me like a rag doll, but I reckon I landed that way, too. Probably saved me a broken bone or two." He clapped his hand on one useless leg. "Not that I'd have noticed."

Harlan looked again at the wheelchair. The control panel had been damaged by the impact, but the wheels and frame looked surprisingly sturdy. "Let's get you into the chair and see if we can't do this the old-fashioned way."

He picked up Bart and set him in the wheelchair, taking another chance to look him over. Bart's well-seamed face was scraped and dirty, but he didn't seem to have any worrisome injuries, to Harlan's relief.

"Quit lookin' at me like I'm about to keel over any minute," Bart groused.

Harlan bit back a grin. "Let's go check on Lila."

The wheelchair wasn't easy to push over the uneven, grassy terrain, especially with Harlan's hand starting to ache as if he'd taken the shrapnel injury moments earlier rather than months ago. But Harlan was so relieved Bart seemed to be okay that he barely felt the pain.

When they reached the edge of the debris pile, Stacy was crouched outside near the governor, peering through the maze of steel and splintered wood. "It looks as if the main thing trapping her is that crossbeam," Stacy told Harlan as he hunkered down beside her. She pointed to a large steel support bar that once had been one of the stabilizing structures for the dais. It didn't look particularly heavy, but the way the bar was wedged between the ground and clumps of the fallen platform, it wouldn't budge. Lila was effectively pinned in place, unable to move more than a couple of inches in any direction.

"You're a big, strappin' fellow. Can't you move it?" Lila asked.

Harlan smiled. "No, ma'am, I'm afraid it's probably going to have to be cut apart to get you out." Especially with his hand being half-useless.

"What about coming at it from the back side?" Stacy asked. "Lila can't turn around because of the debris blocking her, but if I could crawl in and move some of the looser pieces out of the way—"

"No way I'm letting you go under there," Harlan said.

"Now you've done it," Lila murmured.

"Letting me?" Stacy stared at him as if she couldn't believe what she'd just heard. "Not your call, Mr. McClain. If there's even a chance there's a secondary explosive device—"

"There probably isn't."

"But if there is, and someone timed it to go off when it would do the most damage, the governor needs to be out from under there now." Stacy moved away, peering through the remains of the dais—no doubt in search of the best place to enter the maze of rubble. Harlan didn't know whether she was as crazy as a loon or incredibly brave.

"If I go in here and crawl through that narrow breach over there, I can reach the debris blocking the governor from behind," she said, sparing him a quick look.

He bit back his opinion that she was nuts to even try going into that mess, taking a look at what she was proposing instead. She was right about one thing—the path she'd pointed out definitely appeared to be the best angle of attack, and nobody any bigger than Stacy would be able to navigate the tight space.

But the plan was as risky as hell.

"Stacy, you don't need to take foolish chances here," Lila called, drawing her aide's attention back to her. "They'll get to me sooner or later," the governor added with a wry smile. "One of the perks of the job, you know."

Stacy bent down by the opening to make eye contact with the governor. "Waiting could be dangerous, Lila. We need to get you out of there."

"Think about Zachary, honey."

For a second, Stacy's face seemed to melt, her dark eyes

liquid and soft, making Harlan wonder who the hell Zachary was. Then her shoulders squared, her chin jutted forward and she met Harlan's curious gaze.

"I can do this. The structure isn't going to get any more stable if we wait, and I probably have more close-quarters rescue training than any of these first responders."

Before Harlan could respond, an emergency medical technician rounded the corner and spotted them. His eyes widened as he caught sight of the governor buried under the debris, and he squatted next to Stacy.

"I'm not badly hurt, I don't believe," Lila said in a firm, strong voice that seemed to relieve the EMT. "I'm just stuck."

"I have a plan to get to her," Stacy said. She told the EMT what she had in mind.

Harlan hoped the man would tell her she'd lost her mind—maybe she'd listen to him. But the EMT nodded. "That'll probably work, as long as you don't dislodge anything supporting the pile. I can get you a hard hat and some protective gear—"

"I'll take the hat, but the gear will be too bulky to let me get through there."

"Be right back." The EMT hurried away.

"I thought he was going to tell you to stay out of his way and let him do his job," Harlan murmured.

"He knows me. I gave a cave extraction seminar for the Austin Fire Department a couple of months ago."

Harlan shook his head. "Who *are* you?"

Stacy shot him a faint smile. "I'm the daughter of an Ozark Mountain search and rescue coordinator. I was helping pull people out of caves before I started high school."

"You're sure you want to do this?" Harlan asked.

"Yes." Stacy looked scared but determined. "And we'd better get to it, fast," she added, her gaze sliding past him.

Harlan turned, following her gaze to find a convoy of news vehicles approaching the capitol grounds.

"Get your game face on," Stacy muttered. "We're about to be TV stars." She spotted the EMT returning with a hard hat and hurried to meet him, clearly eager to get to work.

Harlan dragged his attention away from her to watch the approach of the news crews. This whole mess was about to get a thousand times messier.

Right now, he thought, *I'd rather be in Iraq.*

You can do this, Stacy. It's just like a cave.

If a cave were made of twisted steel poles and splintered slabs of wood, that was. And if she were really executing a cave rescue, the hard hat on her head would have a carbide lamp attached, enabling her to see more than three or four feet ahead of her. Instead, it just pinched the scrape on her temple that the EMT had patched up for her before she entered the remains of the dais.

"You okay in there?" Harlan McClain's gravelly drawl sounded as if he were standing a quarter mile away, even though she'd crawled no more than a few yards into the debris field.

"So far," she called back, wincing as her palm pressed down onto something sharp—a piece of metal, she saw, bent out of shape and unrecognizable.

Of course, those adjectives could describe almost everything that lay in crumpled heaps around her. If she hadn't seen the dais in all its bunting-draped glory beforehand, she'd never have recognized what it was in the aftermath of the bomb.

Carefully moving aside several twisted pieces of metal frame blocking her path forward, she called out to Lila. "Still hanging in there with me, Governor?"

"You bet, sugar!"

Stacy smiled. "I'm about ten yards from your position, Governor. You just get ready for your close-up."

"Damn, I left my lipstick in my other purse."

Atta girl, Stacy thought. *That's the woman who's going to be the next President of the United States.*

Carefully, she carved a twisting path for herself through the debris, keeping a mental map in her head. Forward about four yards, then left another three. That should put her in reach of the large chunk of tangled metal pinning Lila in position. If she could clear enough of that mess to free the governor to move around, she could get her out to safety.

"I need a little more line," she called to the EMT holding the safety rope biting into her waist. The line slackened and she moved gingerly forward. Finally, she spotted the governor's wavy blond hair, now ashy from the dust and debris caused by the bomb's destruction.

"I see you, Governor."

"I'm a mess, aren't I?"

Stacy chuckled. "Never." She edged around a pole that leaned at a precarious angle, barely holding up a large piece of the stage that could crash down on top of them at any moment. She cleared the hazard and took a sharp left as planned.

Then she froze.

Strapped to the large chunk of steel that formed the obstacle between her and the governor, an electronic device blinked ominously, its smooth facade attached by colorful wires to what looked like pumpkin-colored bricks.

"Governor, don't move. Not one inch."

"What is it?" Lila asked.

Stacy spotted movement outside the fallen dais, jeans-clad legs moving toward the governor's position. Harlan McClain's rugged face came into view as he hunkered down to get a better look at what was happening. His dark eyes met hers. "Is something wrong?"

Stacy licked her lips. By now, she knew, there must be scores of reporters outside. Whatever she said next could create chaos if she let her rising panic show.

Lowering her voice, keeping the tone as calm as possible, she said, "I think there's a second explosive device. And it looks big. You need to start clearing the area. Now. But try not to start a panic."

Harlan moved quickly, disappearing from her sight. A few seconds later, she saw a rush of movement outside the steel-and-lumber cocoon as the EMTs and bystanders responded to whatever Harlan had told them.

"You need to get out of here," Lila urged, her voice low and serious. "Zachary needs you a hell of a lot more than I do."

"I can't go, Governor," Stacy answered, wishing it weren't true. Lila was right. Zachary needed her, even more than most kids his age. She was his biggest advocate and his most devoted fan. But what she wanted didn't change the facts on the ground. "The bomb squad is going to need me."

"Now you're an explosives expert?" Lila retorted tartly. "Any other hidden talents I should know about?"

"That's not what I mean," Stacy answered bleakly. "There's a support beam between here and there that's about thirty degrees shy of falling over and bringing this whole pile of junk raining down on us. I was barely able to get around it without jarring it out of place."

"What are you saying?" It was Harlan McClain's voice, not Lila's, that answered her. Stacy looked up and found him staring at her with wide, worried eyes.

"I'm saying that maybe the governor and I are small enough to crawl out of here without bringing this pile of junk down, but I don't think a man could make it through safely—certainly not wearing a bomb-resistant suit." She tamped down the panic rising in her throat. "I don't think there's going to be any way to disarm this bomb without me."

Chapter Two

Stacy Giordano was right about one thing, Harlan decided, peering up at the slab of wood and steel propped up precariously by the tilting support beam Stacy had described. There was no way anyone bigger than a medium-size woman would ever get through the narrow gap between the beam and another pile of teetering debris without bringing everything crashing down on top of the whole pile.

She appeared in the space ahead of him, considerably grimier than she'd looked when she entered. As she reached him, she held out her cell phone. There was a photo called up on the phone's small display window. "This is the device."

He took care not to touch the teetering support pole as he took the phone from her and looked at the image on the display window. He tried not to react as he saw the orange bricklike cakes of material attached to the bomb. "Semtex," he said aloud. "Industrial grade—not that it makes much difference."

"That's bad, isn't it?"

He nodded. "Bomb squad's on the way. They'll have some ideas about what to do."

Her dark eyes met his. "Get out of here, Mr. McClain. The last thing the rescue team needs is one more person to have to dig out of here."

"You need to get out of there, too."

She shook her head. "If there's any way to defuse the bomb, they'll need me to do it. And the more we move around in here, the more likely we are to dislodge something that'll bring everything crashing down around us. Just go back outside and make sure Mr. Bellows is okay."

"Bart's fine. One of our guys is here—Parker McKenna— you know him?"

She nodded. "He and Bailey just got engaged."

Poor fool, Harlan added silently. Marriage was a sucker's game. "He got Bart and Bailey out of here." Bailey Lockhart hadn't wanted to leave her mother, but Parker had convinced her that the governor would be a lot less stressed out if she knew her daughter was safe.

"Good. Now you get out of here, too," Stacy said.

"Mister, you need to clear out of here and let us do what needs doing," a man barked from somewhere behind Harlan. He turned and saw a uniformed police officer peering through the maze stretching out a few yards behind him.

"You can't go past this spot," Harlan called back to the officer, tersely explaining the problem. "I think anything you try to do to shore it up will just bring it down."

"Who are you?" the officer asked.

"Harlan McClain. I'm with the governor's party." It was close enough to the truth; he was with Bart, who was part of the governor's entourage. "I work with a company who provides the governor with security," he added, figuring a little more embellishment couldn't hurt. For reasons he couldn't quite define, he was reluctant to leave Stacy on her own in this hazardous maze.

He turned around to look at her, but she was already crawling back toward the governor's position. He sighed, frustrated and worried.

"I'm still going to need to get in there, even if I can't move past that support beam," the officer behind him called out in a reasonable tone. "I need to get closer to the bomb if I'm going to help your friend disarm it."

He was right. Harlan was just in the way at this point. He started crawling back out of the hole, emerging on the outside a few seconds later to find himself surrounded by bomb squad members. They were already assessing the debris pile to see if there was a better way to the bomb site.

"There's a whole lot of junk in there ready to fall down on top of you," Harlan warned the one who seemed to be in charge. He showed the man the cell phone photo from Stacy. "Here's a picture of the bomb."

The bomb tech frowned. "Semtex. Radio controlled, if I had to guess."

"Which may mean he's around here somewhere, waiting to send a signal," Harlan said. At the bomb tech's odd look, he added, "Three stints in Iraq."

"Ah." The bomb tech nodded. "It's probably not going to blow if someone touches it—there don't appear to be any trip wires. I think what we have to do is send in a blast blanket to the aide—"

"Stacy Giordano," Harlan supplied.

"Ms. Giordano can detach the bomb—looks like it's just taped to the post—and cover it with the blast blanket. We've got one that has a radio frequency jammer built in. It ought to block any remote signal he tries to send."

"If he's watching, he might send the signal as soon as he spots the blanket."

"We can hide the blanket in something else so he doesn't know we're taking it in," the bomb tech suggested. "We could send in a protective suit and shield the blanket with that."

"I'll take it in," Harlan suggested. "Whoever's watching will be less suspicious of me than of you guys. Plus, I know how the blast blanket works, so I can talk her through it."

The bomb tech frowned, as if he were considering arguing. But finally he nodded. "Just tell her to make sure the yellow side is down."

Harlan nodded.

The minute and a half it took for the bomb squad technicians to surreptitiously hide the blast blanket bag between the folds of the bomb suit seemed to drag on forever. Harlan found himself scanning the area the whole time, wondering if the bomber was watching him at that very moment.

Large numbers of police had finally arrived, keeping the curious onlookers away from the blast area, but a radio signal wouldn't have to come from nearby to do the job. The bomb squad couldn't run full force radio jammers now because it would interfere with the communications between the first responders, a potentially disastrous scenario.

So until Stacy could get that blanket wrapped around the bomb, the bomber had all the time in the world to make his move.

What was the bomber waiting for, anyway? The governor was a sitting duck. He could have already set off the second blast, the second it was clear that she was still alive.

Why hadn't the bomber made his move?

"All set." The bomb tech interrupted Harlan's musings, handing him the bomb suit. He made sure Harlan had a tight grip on the handle of the blast blanket bag peeking out through a space in the suit and nodded for him to go back into the maze. "I'll go around and tell Ms. Giordano what we're doing."

As soon as Harlan was pretty sure he was no longer visible to anyone other than people standing right outside the debris pile, he dropped the suit and pulled out the blast blanket contained in a nylon bag about the size of an artist's portfolio. He hurried as quickly as he dared to the teetering support pole and found Stacy already waiting for him, the bomb lying next to her on the grass.

Somehow, he hadn't expected her to bring the bomb with her. But it was probably smart—the area where she now crouched was about as wide a space as she'd find under the fallen platform.

"Here, let me help you get the blanket through," she said, her dark eyes wide with terror but her chin squared with determination. Once again, Harlan had to give her extra points for sheer guts.

He helped her slide the bag through the narrow space between the sagging pole and the debris field blocking wider access, taking care not to let anything touch the pole.

Once Stacy had the bag clear of the pole, she looked back at Harlan. "What do I do?"

"Inside is a blanket and a smaller collar." He watched as she unzipped the bag and pulled out the contents. "Wrap that collar around the bomb without letting it touch it. Use the Velcro fasteners to close it."

As he took her through the steps of shielding the bomb with the blanket, he was struck by how calmly she was following his orders. Her hands shook a little, but she managed to do everything right the first time. Within a few minutes, the bomb was covered by the blast blanket and the low-frequency radio jammer was working.

Harlan released a sigh of relief. "Go see if you can get the governor out. I'll wait here."

He found himself staring at the dark blue blanket lying on the ground on the other side of the narrow gap, sweat dripping down his forehead. He'd seen an earlier version of the blanket used in Iraq, one with passive rather than active radio jamming capabilities. Most of the time, it had worked.

Once, it hadn't, and he had the shrapnel scars on his trigger hand to show for it. That and an honorable discharge from the Marine Corps that amounted to "Thanks for your service—now get lost."

He heard the sound of movement from the direction in which Stacy had disappeared. A few seconds later, the governor's pale, perspiring face appeared in the gloom. She managed a quick smile as she caught sight of Harlan watching her through the narrow gap.

"You're a hell of a lot more handsome than I remembered," she said with a weak chuckle.

"Clearly you need immediate medical attention," Harlan responded in a teasing tone, relieved to see the governor was able to move around under her own steam.

Bringing up the rear, Stacy Giordano looked wiped out, as if only her determination to help the governor escape had been holding her together over the past hour.

Gingerly, the governor slipped through the narrow gap, careful to avoid the precarious support beam. Harlan didn't even have to call for help—one of the EMTs hurried inside and took charge of the governor, helping her out of the ruins.

Harlan turned to look after Stacy Giordano, catching her as she tripped and swayed precariously close to the slanting pole. Her fingers tangled in the fabric of his shirt, and her dark eyes flickered up to meet his.

The air between them heated, so volatile that Harlan wondered, for a crazy second, if it was enough to set off the bomb they'd so carefully neutralized.

Then Stacy found her balance and let go of his shirt. The tension eased, though it didn't dissipate completely. She thanked him politely in a low, raspy voice and headed for the opening, leaving him to follow behind her.

Outside, the police took over, whisking them out of the blast area and into a squad car parked a safe distance away. Stacy closed her hand around Harlan's arm, reigniting the spark between them for a moment. "I should be with the governor."

He looked down at her hand. Her fingers were slim and small, neatly manicured, though several nails were now broken and ragged from the ordeal. He remembered his first sight of her earlier that day as she was helping the governor prepare for her announcement. The pale gray blouse that was now streaked with blood and grime had been spotless and crisp, businesslike yet still fiercely feminine.

Her dark hair had been up, also, he realized. Coiled at the base of her neck, not loose and tangled as it was now. And she'd had a dark gray jacket to go with her matching trousers, buttoned up and looking every bit the poised, perfect government aide—nothing like the lioness who'd just saved at least a dozen lives with her show of bravery.

"They won't let you see her until they check her out," he responded. "You know the governor's going to get the full package of tests. Better for us to get our statements to the police over with, don't you think? We'll probably get back to the hospital before she's even done."

He turned out to be right. It didn't take long for the police to realize Harlan and Stacy didn't have much to add to what Parker McKenna and Bart Bellows had already told the police about what happened that day. Harlan found he had several of the same questions the police did about the bombing. For starters, why had the first bomb been so low-impact? It had been large enough to take down the dais and blast deadly shrapnel through the surrounding crowd, but there had been minimal impact to the area beyond the platform where the governor had given her speech.

"If the first bomb was so small, why was the second one so much bigger?" Stacy asked another of his questions aloud later as they were on the way to the hospital in the back of a detective's sedan.

Damned good question, Harlan thought. "Maybe they were supposed to go off at the same time and something blocked the signal to the second device. Bomb squad will tell us more."

"Maybe." Stacy didn't sound as if the explanation appeased her curiosity. "Have you heard any news from the hospital?"

"Not a word."

"I hope they're still doing well," she murmured, gazing out the window at the sprawling campus of the University of Texas. Her profile looked pale and fragile, though Harlan knew now that she was a lot tougher than she looked.

"Did you get to call Zachary?" he asked aloud, wondering if she'd spill the beans about who the mysterious Zachary was to her.

She slanted a quick look his way. "I did. He hadn't heard anything about what happened, so he wasn't worried."

"Good," Harlan said, although he wondered how anyone with access to a radio or television could have missed the news about what happened at the capitol.

At the hospital, Parker McKenna was waiting for them in the lobby. "We're all upstairs waiting for more word," Parker told Harlan. "They've done a few tests, but so far everything's looking good. They think she has a mild concussion, so they're going to want to keep her here overnight."

"What about Bart?"

"Him, too. He doesn't seem to have sustained any real injuries—pretty miraculous if you ask me." Parker pushed the button for the fourth floor. "They're going to move Lila into her own room on the fourth floor as soon as they finish the last tests, so we're all gathering in the fourth floor waiting area until they've brought her up."

In the waiting room, Bailey and her sister Chloe sat talking to each other. They both looked up as Harlan, Parker and Stacy entered. Bailey's eyes went soft at the sight of her fiancé, while Chloe Lockhart's baby blues hardened at the sight of Harlan. She wasn't exactly his biggest fan after his stint as her bodyguard a few months back.

"Oh, look. It's Dirty Harry." She greeted him with a roll of her eyes.

"Nice seeing you again, Chloe. Like the hair."

Chloe's right hand went defensively to her spiky pink-streaked hair. "I needed a change."

Bailey pulled away from Parker's hug and reached out to touch Stacy's arm. "Mom told us everything you did for her back there. I don't even know how to start thanking you."

"Thank the Austin bomb squad," Stacy said, looking uncomfortable at the praise.

"I will, but I'm not through thanking you," Bailey said with a smile. "Listen, is there anything I can do for you?"

"I should get busy booking rooms for everyone who's staying overnight," Stacy murmured, looking as if the last thing she was capable of doing was playing social secretary for the governor's entourage. But Harlan supposed that was her job, and the explosion had certainly put a kink in the plans for everyone to hop aboard the governor's private jet and fly back to her home base of Freedom, Texas.

"Why don't you let me do that for you?" Chloe Lockhart suggested in a gentle tone that caught Harlan by surprise. He was used to sarcasm and petulance from the governor's rebellious youngest child.

"No," Stacy snapped, making Chloe flinch. Looking horrified by her own rudeness, Stacy immediately added, "I'm so sorry. I guess I'm still a little stressed."

"Understandable," Chloe answered, her voice sympathetic.

"I just have everything I'd need to get this done on my phone," Stacy added. "Plus, I could really use the distraction." She flashed Bailey and Chloe a faint smile and headed out the door to the courtyard outside the waiting room. Once the door closed behind her, she pulled out her phone and seemed to get right to work.

Harlan watched her, a little worried by the pallor of her face and the way her back bowed with sheer exhaustion.

What if she'd sustained an injury worse than just the scrape to her head? She could be bleeding internally, for all they knew. The EMTs had barely spared a minute to slap a bandage on her head.

"Did the police tell you anything new?" Parker McKenna's question forced Harlan's attention away from Stacy.

With an apologetic look at Bailey, Harlan drew Parker off to the side.

"I'll tell her what we're talking about later, you know," Parker murmured.

Harlan barely kept himself from rolling his eyes. Half the guys at Corps Security and Investigation were sappy in love these days. It was becoming an epidemic—one Harlan had no intention of getting sucked into. His ex-wife had done an excellent job of immunizing him against the love bug. He might thank her one of these days, if he ever decided to speak to her again.

"Regardless, the governor's daughters don't need to hear us analyzing who might want to blow up their mother and why," he said aloud to Parker. "The situation's scary enough."

"Tell me about it," Parker growled. "I thought when we caught Frank Dorian, this kind of thing was over."

"What's the chance that Dorian had an accomplice we don't know about?"

"Believe me, I've been thinking about that myself," Parker admitted. "But it just doesn't make sense. Dorian's motive was so personal. It's not like he's going to pass on his obsession to some random bomber he found in the phone book."

Harlan knew Parker was right. Frank Dorian had blamed Lila Lockhart for her decision not to pardon his brother, who'd been on Texas's death row. His brother's execution had been too much for Dorian's brokenhearted mother, and Dorian blamed Lila for her death, as well. His decision to go after the governor had been deeply personal rather than political, and his arrest had put an end to the threats against the governor and her family.

But at least it would have been a place to start looking.

Instead, they didn't have a clue who'd planted the two bombs at the capitol today. People had been killed. Even more had been injured, some critically.

And for what? Just because Lila Lockhart had decided she wasn't through serving her country?

The world was a crazy, crazy place.

Harlan's gaze drifted toward the large plate glass window looking out on the concrete courtyard, where he'd last seen Stacy Giordano. She was no longer talking on the phone, nor had she reentered the hospital waiting room. Instead, she sat on one of the three concrete benches loosely circling a large potted evergreen tree, her back to the window. Her hunched shoulders and lowered head made her look small and fragile.

Harlan's gut tightened with concern.

"Is she okay?" Parker's gaze had followed Harlan's, settling on Stacy's slender form.

"She had a scrape on her head, but the EMT didn't seem to think it amounted to much." Of course, in the middle of all the chaos, the paramedic hadn't exactly spent much time checking her out. "I'll go check on her."

As he stepped out onto the narrow fourth floor terrace,

Stacy turned to see who had disturbed her solitude. In her pale face, her eyes looked big and haunted. "Has something happened?" she asked, her voice tinged with alarm.

"No. I just wanted to check on you." He sat on one of the adjacent benches, squelching the urge to reach out and touch her folded hands. "You look tired."

"Long day," she murmured with a hint of wry humor.

"Hellish day," he agreed. "Did you manage to get all your calls made?"

"I think so." The humor in her eyes faded. "I just wish I were home."

"I bet your husband does, too." Even as the words escaped his lips, Harlan knew he was fishing for information about her marital status. He gave himself a mental kick.

She grimaced. "No. No husband."

He quirked an eyebrow. "Um, sorry?"

She flashed a quick, humorless grin. "No, not sorry."

So, another wounded warrior back from the marital battlefield? That was even more dangerous.

Her smile faded as quickly as it had risen. "Do we have a death tally from the blast yet?"

He shook his head. "I found two D.O.A. at the scene. At least two more who were in really bad shape."

Her chin trembled and a sheen of moisture filled her dark eyes. "Damn it."

The urge to pull her into a hug caught him off guard. He wasn't a demonstrative guy. He didn't do tea and sympathy. But something about Stacy Giordano's vulnerability punched him right in the gut. He wanted to make things better for her.

And that scared the hell out of him.

"I'd better go see if Lila's been asking for me." Stacy pushed herself off the bench, wincing a little as if the movement caused her pain.

Harlan couldn't stop himself from reaching out to steady her, his fingers closing around her upper arm. Her gaze shot up, a quizzical look in her eyes, and for a second, he felt as if his whole body had turned to liquid.

Heat quickly eclipsed that melting sensation. He pulled his hand back, disturbed by his reaction to her.

The door from the waiting room opened, and Parker stood in the doorway, his expression grim. "I just got a call from Wade," he said. "Frank Dorian's dead."

Chapter Three

The governor stayed on the phone for most of the very early flight home from Austin the next morning, giving Stacy time to decompress from the past twenty-four hours. Staying busy arranging for the governor's entourage to stay in Austin overnight had helped fill her afternoon, and the temporary drama of learning about Frank Dorian's jailhouse death had occupied most of the early evening, as Bailey Lockhart's fiancé, Parker McKenna, and his colleague Harlan McClain had stayed in constant touch with their counterparts at the Corps Security and Investigations office in Freedom, relaying information as it trickled in.

All evidence pointed to suicide—Dorian had fashioned a noose from his jail-issued shirt and hung himself from the bars of his cell—but Bart Bellows had selected the men who worked at CSI because they were thorough and resourceful. Stacy had tried not to eavesdrop on their conversations, but she'd gleaned enough to know that one of the CSI agents had a contact at the Freedom Police Department who was keeping them apprised of the department's investigation. If there was anything strange about Dorian's death, the agents of CSI were determined to figure out what it was and what, if anything, it had to do with the attack on the governor.

Stacy had found herself growing more and more impressed with the two CSI agents as the evening went on.

She knew from Bailey that Corps Security and Investigations was made up of former military men. Parker had been an Army Captain, and it showed. He'd been a huge help in keeping everyone in the governor's entourage calm and focused.

She wasn't sure what branch of the military Harlan McClain had been part of. He wore his sandy brown hair short, but so did most of the other former military men she knew. He was hard-muscled, as she'd learned when she'd practically collapsed in his arms after tripping on their way out of the debris field. Clearly he'd kept himself in shape since parting company with whatever military branch he'd served in.

He smelled good, too, she thought, even when sweating out a bomb scare. He didn't wear cologne like a lot of men, including her ex-husband, did. He smelled of good old soap and water, a light, clean scent that probably wouldn't have smelled masculine on anyone else.

Harlan McClain was masculine to the core. It had showed in how he'd dealt with the aftermath of the bombing—taking charge, keeping things moving. He'd tended to the dead and wounded, delegated authority to others as needed, and jumped right in to help Stacy when they found the governor buried under the rubble.

Very different from her ex-husband, Anthony, who'd never met a problem he couldn't analyze to death.

"Looking forward to seeing Zachary?" Lila murmured, drawing Stacy's attention back to the cabin of the small jet.

"Yes," she answered, even if there was a small part of her that was dreading seeing her son after the unexpected night away from home. Zachary hated changes to his routine, so he'd probably given poor Charlotte a hard time last night. Stacy almost envied Charlotte—at least a tantrum was a response. When Zachary was immersed in his own little world—a frequent event—he barely acknowledged Stacy's presence.

They arrived in Freedom a little after 7:00 a.m. Stacy stayed with the governor for a few minutes, going over the changes to Lila's schedule arranged in response to the events in Austin and planning ahead for a couple of television interviews to let the people of Texas see that the governor was ready to finish out her term with her usual sass and vigor.

Finally, Lila told her to take the rest of the morning off, but to come back to the ranch house for lunch. "I have something else I need to discuss with you."

With curiosity niggling at the back of her brain, Stacy walked to the ranch guesthouse she shared with her son. She found Charlotte Manning in the middle of helping Zachary find a pair of socks to wear to school.

Charlotte looked surprised to see her. "How'd the governor get the hospital to let her go so early?"

"You know how the governor is. What doctor was going to say no?" Stacy smiled at Zachary, who looked up at her for a second, then looked away, showing no sign of interest.

He went back to his search, sorting through the socks to find the blue pair. Tuesday meant the blue socks. Always.

A cold ache settled in her chest. After a year and a half of trying to come to terms with Zachary's condition, she now realized she wasn't ever going to get used to it. She'd spent every available hour researching Asperger's syndrome, reading books, blogs, dry medical journal articles and heartfelt newspaper stories from parents of aspies, as people with Asperger's syndrome referred to themselves. She'd come across a blog by a young college student who had Asperger's and found some comfort in how grounded the young woman seemed to be, despite her different way of experiencing life, but ultimately, she'd had to accept that life with her beautiful son would be a series of never-ending challenges.

He'd have trouble making friends. He might never fall in love and have a life partner. He might find a job he loved but he just as easily might not. She'd fight with everything inside her to help him reach his full potential, but it was impossible to tell what that potential might be right now, when he was barely old enough to tie his shoes on his own.

"The Arabian horse has a concave nose," Zachary announced, still looking at the sock drawer. He reached in and extracted the blue socks, showing no sense of triumph as he pulled the blue socks onto his small feet. "The Morgan horse is the first American breed of horse to survive to this day."

"He's been reading his horse book again?" Stacy asked Charlotte.

Charlotte nodded, her shaggy red hair bouncing with the movement. "He was pretty insistent about reading it to me at bedtime. His reading is getting to be downright amazing."

"I know he must have been disappointed not to take a riding lesson yesterday." Stacy had been taking him for lessons every Monday and Thursday for a few weeks now. Lindsay Kemp at the Long K Ranch had started giving riding lessons to disabled children a few years ago. While Zachary's problems were more developmental than physical, riding at the Long K had turned out to be good therapy for him. He loved horses enough to make the effort to interact with Lindsay in order to learn better how to deal with the horses.

Maybe she could sneak him down to the governor's stables later this week. One of the groomsmen there, Trevor Lewis, had let Zachary ride one of the governor's gentler horses a few times before. He seemed to know a little about Asperger's syndrome—something about a cousin who had it—and he accepted Zachary's idiosyncrasies without making a big deal about it.

"Charlotte, I'll finish up getting him ready for school. You go ahead—I know you need to get there earlier than the children do."

Charlotte taught Zachary and a small number of other students with learning challenges. One of the draws for Stacy when she was considering taking the job with the governor was the Cradle to Crayons day care. The reputation of its special education curriculum was excellent. Everyone Stacy had asked about the school had concurred—Zachary couldn't ask for a better learning environment.

These days, Zachary was her reason for everything she did.

Charlotte had been a godsend. Once she'd learned about Zachary's Asperger's syndrome, she'd gone to work studying up on the condition and how best to work around his lack of social skills to make sure he was prepared for elementary school when the time came.

Stacy wasn't sure she was ready to think that far ahead.

"He's had breakfast, but he hasn't brushed his teeth," Charlotte warned. "His lunch is packed already—"

Stacy gave her an impulsive hug. "I don't know how to thank you for this. Just tell me what I owe you."

"Work in a couple of hours volunteering at the school over the next few weeks and we'll call it even," Charlotte said. "It was good for me to do this. It gave me a better understanding of how to deal with Zachary during school hours. It's like on-the-job training."

Stacy walked Charlotte to the door. "I'll work out a volunteer schedule as soon as I get the governor settled back into some sort of routine."

"I imagine that'll take some doing," Charlotte said with a wry grin as she headed out the door.

You have no idea, Stacy thought, closing the door behind Charlotte.

"What do you think?" Harlan leaned over Vince Russo's shoulder, growing impatient with his fellow agent's continuing silence. Vince was Corps Security and Investigation's go-to guy when it came to explosives. If anyone could tell them anything interesting about the undetonated bomb Stacy had found in the debris, it was Vince.

"It's basically an Iraqi-style IED," Vince answered flatly.

Harlan released a long, slow breath. He'd thought so as well, at first glance, though his experience with explosives hadn't been as hands-on as Vince's had been. A former navy SEAL, Vince had set—and defused—his share of explosive devices during his time in Iraq.

"Can you tell anything else about it?"

"It's a common make of phone—something you could find in just about any store in America. The cops will be able to see if the phone can be traced to anyone." Vince looked up at Harlan. "It's not likely. The device is fairly cobbled together, but whoever made it knew what he was doing. It's a miracle he didn't set it off before the bomb squad got there to disarm it."

"I was wondering about that myself—" The door to the agents' bull pen opened and Parker McKenna wheeled Bart Bellows through the door in a manual wheelchair.

Vince and Harlan both rose to greet their boss, hurrying to shake his hand.

"Aren't you still supposed to be in the hospital?" Harlan asked, worried about how pale the older man looked.

"Hell, if Lila can talk her way out of a hospital bed, I'll be damned if I'm going to laze about in Austin all day." Bart directed his sharp blue-eyed gaze at Harlan, nodding his head toward the corner. "Let's talk, McClain."

Harlan wheeled Bart with him to the corner, away from the other agents. "What's up?"

"The governor asked me to get you to her ranch for lunch."

"Why?"

"I reckon she might want to thank you again in person."

Harlan shook his head. "I didn't do much of anything. She should thank her aide. She's the one who crawled into that maze and got things done."

He'd found it hard to get Stacy Giordano off his mind over the past few hours. Her gritty courage had impressed the hell out of him, but it was the pale, troubled expression on her face when he'd left her there at the hospital to start the long drive home to Freedom that had stuck with him through the intervening hours. He knew next to nothing about her, really, but he had a gut-level sense that she was a woman under an enormous amount of pressure beyond her demanding job.

Stop it. She's not your problem. You have all the problems you need.

"Well, be that as it may, she asked for you to be there, and you're going. Because that woman may well be the next president of the United States, and you don't say no to someone who might wield that sort of power someday."

"Fine. I'm up for a free lunch." It would be a real pleasure to eat something that didn't come straight out of a can or a microwave plate.

Bart gave a satisfied nod and started wheeling himself back to where the other men had gathered around Vince's computer, looking at the bomb.

Harlan joined them, catching the tail end of what Vince was telling Parker. "The setup is pretty typical of what the *al Antqam* were using a few years back."

"*Al Antqam?*" Bart asked.

"Loosely translated, it means Sons of Vengeance," Harlan answered, not looking away from the computer screen. "They were a particularly vicious sect working out of the Anbar Province. Gave us a whole lot of trouble for a while."

"I know that." Bart's voice sounded hoarse.

Harlan looked up and saw that the old man had gone as pale as milk. "Bart, are you okay?"

Bart's eyes darted up to meet Harlan's. "I'm fine." He wheeled his chair toward the door. "I'll be here around eleven-thirty to drive you to the governor's ranch," he called over his shoulder to Harlan. Parker hurried to open the door for him and went with him to the elevator.

"What was that about?" Vince asked Harlan.

Harlan shook his head. "No idea." He didn't know much about Bart beyond the basics—he was a Vietnam vet who'd later joined the CIA and eventually became a defense contractor before he sold out for billions. But that was the sort of stuff he could have found out by going on the internet.

Parker returned a few minutes later, looking troubled. "I'm not sure Bart should have left the hospital. His hands were shaking like crazy."

"What do you know about Bart's history?" Harlan asked.

Parker shrugged. "Just what he told me when he hired me. Which wasn't much."

"Same here," Vince agreed.

"I don't think he's sick," Harlan said. "I think what we were talking about disturbed him."

"What were we talking about—the bomb?" Vince asked.

"We were talking about *al Antqam*," Harlan said, remembering the tone of Bart's voice when he'd echoed Harlan's words. Before he'd looked up to see Bart's ashen face, he'd thought Bart had simply been asking a question.

Now he wondered if it was more than that.

"Well, you're about to rub elbows with the old man during lunch," Vince said with a shrug. "Why don't you ask him?"

Harlan planned to do just that. But when Bart's long black

Cadillac arrived in front of the CSI headquarters shortly after eleven, the old man wasn't inside.

"Where's Bart?" Harlan asked the driver as he slid into the front passenger seat.

"He went on ahead earlier to talk to the governor." The driver, a grizzled old former cowboy named Dalton Hicks, waited for Harlan to buckle his seat belt before he entered the light traffic. "Said he'd see you there."

Harlan knew from listening to Bailey Lockhart talk that Twin Harts Ranch was still a working cattle ranch, but he had to admit, if he hadn't known that already, he'd never have guessed it by looking at the imposing two-story white villa that served as the governor's home. Sugar-white columns flanked the portico, and a long outside corridor, shaded by another portico with columns, extended nearly the length of the house.

"Nice, huh?" Hicks drawled as he pulled up in front of the entrance. "Wait till you see the inside."

Harlan unfolded himself from the Cadillac and walked to the door. Beneath his feet, the narrow walkway was polished marble, making him wish he could take off his dusty boots to keep from marring the shiny surface.

He didn't see a doorbell, so he rapped the heavy brass knocker against the white door. A pair of glass insets reflected his own face back to him, preventing him from seeing inside. But he heard movement, the flurry of footsteps, and the door swung open wide.

It was the governor herself who answered the door, to his surprise. "Welcome, Mr. McClain. So nice to see you again."

"Should you be answering the door yourself?" he couldn't help asking as he followed her through a large, ornate foyer into a hallway that was only slightly narrower. "Someone just tried to kill you."

She glanced over her shoulder at him. "I saw who was there. And the glass in the door is bullet-resistant." Her lips curved. "Besides, the Texas State Troopers in my security detail have been tracking your arrival since you drove onto Twin Harts land ten minutes ago."

He should have known. He supposed a woman of Lila Lockhart's power and controversial outspokenness couldn't thrive this long in a volatile political climate without knowing how to take a few precautions to protect herself.

The governor led him into a cozy sitting room filled with large, dark-wood furniture and colorful woven rugs. Paneling darkened the walls and gave the place a rustic feeling at odds with the European refinement of the ranch house's exterior.

A woman of many contradictions, Harlan thought as the occupants of the study turned to look at the newcomers.

Bart Bellows was there, his chair parked in front of the large river stone hearth, where golden flames licked lazily at a slab of hickory firewood. He grinned at Harlan as if he were keeping a juicy secret. Next to Bart, a sandy-haired man wearing a neat business suit watched Harlan's approach with an oddly speculative gleam in his blue eyes.

And in an armchair adjacent to the stranger, Stacy Giordano sat quietly, her gaze watchful and wary.

"Stacy, I'm sure you remember Mr. McClain," the governor said, waving for Harlan to sit on the small sofa across from Stacy. Stacy flashed him a quick smile as he sat, briefly transforming her features as if a beam of sunlight had fallen across her face. The smile faded quickly, her gaze returning to Lila's face as the governor sat beside Harlan on the sofa.

"And this is Greg Merritt," the governor added, waving toward the stranger. "He's going to be my campaign manager. Greg, this is the man I was telling you about, Harlan McClain."

Merritt rose and extended his hand to Harlan. He spoke with a mild Texas twang. "Happy to meet you, Mr. McClain. The governor tells me you were instrumental in saving her life yesterday. We're all very grateful."

"Just call me Harlan," he said, uncomfortable with the praise considering how little he'd done compared to Stacy. But before he could protest, the governor cut in.

"I am deeply grateful to you, Mr.— Harlan." The governor smiled, then turned to look at Stacy. Her smile grew warmer. "And to you, darlin'. I won't forget what you did for me. But that's not really why I asked the two of you here for lunch." She took a deep breath, as if bracing for what she would say next.

Stacy's gaze briefly connected with Harlan's. He saw a hint of surprise and, unexpectedly, a flicker of dread.

"In two weeks, I intend to hold my first official fundraiser for my presidential campaign. Right here at Twin Harts. I'm going to ask that lovely girl Carrie Rivers to entertain us again." The governor smiled brightly. "It's going to be a party just about as big as Texas. Of course, Stacy will be in charge of bringing the party together. Nobody can get things done for me better than she can."

The dread in Stacy's eyes turned into full-blown panic.

"And you, Harlan, will be in charge of security."

Harlan glanced at Stacy again. Babysitting the governor and her entourage of fans and followers wouldn't normally be at the top of his list of desirable assignments, though he had to admit the recent attempt on Lila Lockhart's life added a little zing of excitement to the prospect.

But working day in and day out with the governor's enigmatic—and intriguing—aide?

Now, *that* might turn out to be a real challenge.

Chapter Four

"I want to go riding, Mommy."

Setting aside her pile of notes, Stacy turned to look into her son's bright blue eyes. He wore an expression she was coming to know well, the "come hell or high water" look he gave her when he was determined to get his way.

"Zachary, I told you I have to work this afternoon." She knew she was fortunate to be able to work from home when necessary. She and Zachary lived in the guesthouse at Twin Harts, so she was only a short walk from the governor's own office at the ranch house.

"I was supposed to go riding Monday, but you changed the plans." He sounded quite put out about it, too.

"Yes, I changed the plans. I told you why I changed them, didn't I? Miss Lila had to visit the capitol, and I had to go with her. Remember?"

And then things blew up, literally, and now I have to work with a big, hard-muscled ex-military man with sexy brown eyes whom I can't stop thinking about no matter how I try.

"You changed the plans, and I didn't get to ride."

"I'm taking you to see Miss Lindsay tomorrow, remember? It's your regular riding lesson."

Zachary's round little face darkened. "You have to take me twice a week. I have to get a riding lesson in before tomorrow. I have to."

Even though his vocal inflections and pronunciation were still those of a child of five, the words he chose and the sentence structure he used were far beyond his years. It was one of a wide range of possible indicators of Asperger's syndrome. So was his dogged obsession with horses.

Some aspies became obsessed with video games. Some focused on planes or trains or cars. Zachary's obsession with horses seemed to date back to the age of three, when her ex-husband's parents had given Zachary a rocking horse for his birthday. That had been shortly after Stacy had started to realize her beautiful, bright son wasn't the same as other children.

He'd been diagnosed with Asperger's a few weeks later. For about three months, she and her ex-husband, Anthony, had struggled against the diagnosis, trying to come up with some other rational explanation for Zachary's developmental difficulties. But all the signs were there, and finally, Stacy had been forced to face the truth. Her son was going to have a radically different life than the one she'd dreamed of when she'd first learned she was having a baby.

She'd accepted the truth. Anthony had not.

"Tell you what," she said, gazing at her son with so much love in her heart she thought it might burst, "I'll see if Mr. Miller can work you in at Miss Lila's stable, okay?"

Zachary cocked his head, as if considering the offer. "Okay. What time?"

She glanced at her watch. It was almost two, and she had at least another hour's worth of calls to make. "How about three? I'll call Mr. Miller and see if he can work you in."

She found the number for the stables and dialed, hoping the affable stable manager would be able to find a gentle horse for Zachary to ride around the paddock for a while this afternoon. If not, the rest of her day was going to be sheer hell.

The stable manager, Cory Miller, answered the phone. He was a gruff old Texan who'd been with the Lockhart family since Lila's daughters and son were children. "Trevor's nearly through with his work for the day—I can have him let Zachary have a ride."

"Thank you so much, Cory!" Stacy nearly melted with relief. Trevor was one of the younger grooms. He seemed to enjoy letting Zachary take rides now and then. Maybe Zachary would settle down now and let her get on with the plans for the governor's fundraiser. "And Cory? Please don't tell the governor about this. I don't want her to think Zachary's getting in anyone's way."

"I don't reckon she'd think that," Cory protested. "But all right, Ms. Stacy. I'll keep it to myself."

Maybe Lila wouldn't think she couldn't handle the job because of Zachary's special needs, but Stacy was in no position to put her job at risk. Lila paid very well, enough to cover the costs of Zachary's weekly therapy sessions. If something happened to change the governor's mind about Stacy's ability to do the job, she didn't know if she'd be able to find another job as flexible and lucrative.

Had she been wrong to believe she could handle a job as demanding as being Lila Lockhart's aide-de-camp?

For a brief while, Lila had even named Stacy campaign manager for her presidential run, until Stacy—and others in the governor's circle of friends—had convinced her that hiring a seasoned political pro was the only smart choice. Though deeply flattered by Lila's confidence in her instincts and skills, Stacy knew her limitations. Lila deserved the best. Greg Merritt was the best.

Despite the daunting list of phone calls Stacy needed to make before Zachary's impromptu riding lesson, she couldn't concentrate. Zachary was being too quiet, so she took a quick break to see where her son had disappeared to.

She found him in his bedroom, riding the rocking horse his grandparents had given him. He chattered quietly to the toy, as if giving it commands. At five, he dwarfed the toddler's toy, the sight comical enough to make Stacy smile.

He looked up at the sound of her footsteps on the hard-wood floor, then resumed his play. No expression of welcome. No smile. Not even a grin of embarrassment at being caught playing with a baby toy.

Tears stung her eyes, but she fought them off, even though he wouldn't react to them anyway.

"Is it time to go?" he asked, not taking his eyes off the rocking horse.

"Not yet." She retreated from the room and let the burning tears fall, even though she knew she'd probably regret the show of weakness later, not being the sort of person who gave in to self-pity. But after the past few days, she supposed she could cut herself some slack.

It wasn't as if the next couple of weeks were going to be any less stressful, after all. Between preparing for the fundraiser and working long and no doubt demanding hours with Harlan McClain, the next couple of weeks would be like living in a pressure cooker.

And if she wasn't careful, the whole situation just might blow up on her. Because there was something about Harlan McClain that seemed to press all her buttons, good and bad.

When Anthony left, she'd thought her disillusionment and sense of betrayal had immunized her against the charms of any male besides Zachary. But even in the middle of a life-and-death situation in Austin, something about Harlan McClain had made its way past the walls she'd spent the past year and half building to keep herself and Zachary safe from any more unnecessary disappointments.

There had even been that moment, brief but powerful, when she'd literally fallen into his arms and realized that she could still feel wildly attracted to a man despite her determination to never be the fool again.

She'd have to be very careful not to let Harlan McClain slip through her defenses again.

THE GOVERNOR HAD GIVEN HARLAN a day off before starting work on the security plans for the fundraiser. He supposed she thought he'd need to tie up any loose ends in his personal life, since she clearly expected him to spend most of his waking hours at the ranch, coordinating the event. But he didn't have any loose ends to tie up. His life these days was blissfully uncomplicated—no wife, no kids, no one to answer to besides Bart Bellows and his fellow agents at CSI.

Yeah, life was just a big ol' bowl of cherries.

Well, except for the fact that the dream home he'd spent so much time planning for and saving for had gone to his ex in the divorce. Never mind that Alexis had been the one getting naked with the contractor—her daddy was a golfing buddy of the divorce court judge, and if that hadn't been enough, the high-priced Atlanta lawyer she'd hired somehow managed to twist Harlan's years of outstanding service in the Marine Corps into de facto abandonment of his wife and their marriage.

Goodbye, two-story farmhouse in Walnut Grove, Georgia. Hello, three-room man-cave in Freedom, Texas, with the thrift-store furnishings and only the big-screen TV he'd eked out of the divorce settlement to give him any sense of his old life following him into his new one.

Well, there was also his trusty old Ford F-10 pickup. Alexis never liked the truck, and he supposed he should just be glad she got all the vindictiveness out of her system by taking the house.

A quick rap on the door of his apartment dragged him out of his grim funk. Matt Soarez stood outside, holding a pink envelope. One black eyebrow arched upward. "It's for you."

Harlan took the envelope. It had his name written on the outside in a familiar script and smelled of gardenias.

Well, hell.

"Holding out on us, McClain?" Soarez grinned broadly. "Who's the lady?"

"She's no lady." Harlan grimaced. "She's my ex-wife."

Soarez winced. "I thought she was back in Georgia."

"So did I." Harlan frowned at the pink envelope. "Where did you find this?"

"In front of my door." Matt lived in the next apartment to his own. "I just got home from lunch at Talk of the Town."

Harlan glanced at his watch. It was after three. He shot Soarez a skeptical look.

"Hey, it's my day off," Soarez said with a grin. "Faith and I have plans to make, you know."

"Plans for the wedding?" Not that Harlan cared about things like weddings or marriage or that mewling little baby girl of Faith Scott's that Soarez was so sappy over. But anything to keep from opening the envelope from Alexis.

"Well, yeah, that, too." Soarez's grin widened further. "But first, we're moving in together."

Not what Harlan expected, though it shouldn't have come as a surprise. Soarez had been spending most of his hours away from work over at Faith's place anyway. He lived right down the hall from Harlan, but Harlan hardly ever saw him outside of work anymore. "When's that going to happen?"

"This weekend, unless something comes up at the agency." Soarez's dark eyes glittered with happiness. "I get to be a full-time daddy to Kayleigh."

Harlan bit back the snarky reply teetering on the edge of his tongue. "You'll enjoy that."

Soarez didn't miss the lack of enthusiasm. "Not all women are lying cheats, Georgia. Give it a little time. Maybe you'll find a girl like Faith, too."

Harlan didn't want a girl like Faith. He didn't want a woman in his life at all. In his bed? Sure. But beyond that, women were nothing but trouble.

Soarez shrugged. "Well, I'll leave you to the she-beast's letter." He headed back down the hall to his apartment.

With a heavy sigh, Harlan closed the door behind him, leaning against the solid wood as he contemplated the pink envelope that smelled like gardenias.

What do you want, Alexis?

He ran his finger under the flap, wincing at a paper cut. *Perfect,* he thought, sliding the folded note from the envelope. Pressing his thumb to the nicked finger, he used the other hand to shake open the paper.

I'm in Freedom. Call me. We need to talk. No number written down on the page, so he guessed she still had her old cell phone number.

He crumpled the paper and tossed it in the garbage can in the kitchen, grabbing his jacket. He was halfway to his truck when his curiosity overcame his stubborn pride.

What on God's green earth would Alexis be doing in Texas? He'd known her since they were both twelve years old, and he'd never heard her mention any family here. Certainly not in a tiny dot on the map like Freedom.

Had something happened to someone in her family? Did she need his help with something?

Growling a profanity, he climbed into the truck cab and pulled out his cell phone. She was still on his speed dial, he noticed with a grimace. He punched the code.

She answered on the first ring. "Hey, stranger."

He laid his head back against the headrest. She might be a liar and a cheat, but that sweet magnolia accent still sounded pretty damned good. "What's wrong, Alexis?"

There was a brief pause on the other end of the line. "Nothing's wrong. I just need to talk to you about something."

"Call my lawyer."

"It's not a lawyer kind of topic," she said, impatience adding a hint of spice to that honeyed drawl. "Just come meet me at the Bella Rosa. I'll buy you a cup of coffee."

"Despite your best efforts, I can still buy my own cup of coffee," he replied. "Are you there now?"

"Yes. You'll come?"

"Yes," he said after a long pause. "But this better be important."

"It is," she assured him.

He hung up without responding, muttering a low curse as he realized his nightmare of a marriage had found a way to live on, even after the divorce papers had been signed.

Bella Rosa was a small bistro on the eastern edge of Freedom's town square. It was a few blocks down from Talk of the Town, the friendly little café owned by Matt Soarez's pretty fiancée, Faith. Harlan was glad Alexis had expensive tastes—if he'd met his ex-wife at Talk of the Town, news of the meeting would be all over town by sunset.

Meeting her at Bella Rosa meant the news would take a few more days to circulate, giving him time to come up with a story that didn't make him look like a grade-A sap.

She was sitting at a table near the back, her honey-blond hair twisted into a neat, attractive coil at the base of her neck. She arched one perfect eyebrow at his casual attire—he'd seen no reason to change out of his jeans and golf shirt just to have lunch with his ex-wife—but waved him over.

"What's up?" he asked without preamble, sitting across from her and waving off the waiter who'd practically trailed him to the table.

"You don't want anything to eat?"

"I'm not hungry." Not the exact truth, but he wasn't hungry enough to eat with her. "Just get to the point."

She took a deep breath and folded her neatly manicured hands over each other. "I'm getting remarried."

Harlan wasn't sure what he'd expected her to say, but telling him she was getting married again wasn't it.

"No response?" she asked with a nervous chuckle.

"What's there to say? Congratulations, I guess? Best wishes? I never remember which you say to the bride and which to the groom."

"Thank you." She smiled at him.

"So I guess this takes me off the hook for any more alimony."

"I never wanted you to have to pay alimony. I don't need your money."

"I don't think you ever needed anything from me," he murmured. "Speaking of the groom, I have to admit I'm surprised. I always figured Ted the Contractor as more a fling kind of relationship than anything long-term, but if he makes you happy—"

"I'm not marrying Ted," she said. "I'm marrying Alden."

He stared at her. "Alden? Your fifty-year-old shark of a divorce lawyer Alden?"

"Forty-six," she corrected. "And he's only a shark in the courtroom. He's really very sweet. And attentive."

And I wasn't attentive, Harlan thought. *Of course, I was a little busy at the time, dodging bullets and bombs while fighting for my country, but hey. That's not your problem, is it, sweetheart?*

"How's your hand?" she asked a moment later. He wasn't sure if she asked the question just to break the uncomfortable silence or if she really cared.

He flexed his right hand, where the scar tissue from the shrapnel wounds was still pale and tight, limiting his mobility. "About the same. I think therapy's gotten me about as far as it can. I just have to adjust to the limitations now."

"I'm sorry you were hurt, but I'm glad it got you out of the Marines," Alexis said, her chin held high as if bracing herself for his anger.

"Too bad you didn't wait a few months longer before you slept with the contractor. I'd have had plenty of time to be attentive," he responded.

She looked hurt by his words. He almost felt guilty, until he remembered the humiliation of walking into his bedroom and finding Alexis naked and wrapped around the muscular contractor Harlan had hired to build their dream home.

"I've told you I was sorry you found us that way."

"But not about having sex with the guy behind my back?"

"You know as well as I do our marriage was doomed. We're too different. We want different things out of life."

That much was true. He definitely didn't want to marry a ruthless divorce lawyer. Matter of fact, he didn't want to marry anyone at all. Ever again.

Once was enough.

"You flew all the way to Texas to tell me you were getting married?" he asked. "You could have just called."

"Alden's attending a conference in Lubbock. I thought it would be better to tell you the news face-to-face."

He just looked at her, taking in her prom-queen beauty, which hadn't yet faded with age, and her hopeful expression. She wanted closure. Maybe even absolution.

Would it hurt so much to give it to her?

He forced a smile. "I really do hope you and Alden are happy. And that he stays just as attentive fifty years from now as he is today."

Her smile in return made her look sixteen years old again, bright and beautiful and everything he'd thought he wanted in life. He'd loved her like crazy once.

But not anymore, he realized with a little shiver of relief.

He might still resent her infidelity and her lies, but he didn't really care who she slept with anymore.

I guess that's progress, he thought.

"I hope you find someone, too," she added.

He felt his rising mood deflate again. "I'm not really in the market."

"Just because our marriage didn't work out—"

He stood, looking down at her one last time. "Have a good life, Alexis."

"You, too," she said.

But he was already headed out the door, stepping into the warm midday breeze blowing in over the western plains.

He looked around him, taking in the friendly facades of the shops and businesses that formed the town square. Old cottonwoods and sprawling oaks lined the streets, giving the place the look of an idyllic oasis in the middle of the arid Texas Panhandle.

He'd taken the job Bart Bellows offered because it was a chance to start over, to see what life would be like outside the Marine Corps and his shattered marriage. Freedom seemed like a great place to make a new life—just as in most small towns, it was hard to stay a stranger for long in Freedom.

But Harlan had never felt more alone.

He checked his watch. A little after two. Half of the day spread out ahead of him, barren and daunting.

With a sigh, he pulled out his cell phone and dialed the direct line Lila Lockhart had given him before he left her ranch the night she gave him his new assignment.

He was surprised she answered on the first ring. "Hello, Mr. McClain." Her drawl was warm and amused. "You haven't reconsidered, have you?"

"No, Governor, I haven't. In fact, I'd like to get started today. How quickly can you gather up the staff?"

Chapter Five

Stacy sneaked a glance at her watch. Nearly four. Zachary was probably through with his ride by now.

When was Harlan McClain going to adjourn this meeting?

"Need to be somewhere?" Greg Merritt murmured.

"Nervous habit."

Harlan McClain's eyes narrowed, but he kept speaking. "We're setting up guards at all entry roads. Until the fence is constructed, we've set up checkpoints around the property—on the approach to the guesthouse, the path to the pasture, the main road and the road to the stables. We need to keep track of where everyone is and where you're going."

Great, Stacy thought. *Just great.* She had to go through a checkpoint to pick up her son from his ride?

"I need full cooperation to make this work. One of the best ways we can detect and identify threats to the governor is for the rest of us to stick to the protocols so that the aberrations stand out. Everybody understand?"

There were nods and murmurs of assent. Stacy released a soft sigh of frustration.

"I know these new protocols sound overly restrictive, but they're necessary for the governor's protection. Yours, too. People were killed in Austin. We can't let that happen here. Not on our watch."

Stacy felt guilty for feeling frustrated, but the facts didn't change her dilemma. She needed to get her son from the stables without going through the security checkpoint Harlan McClain had set up. She didn't want the governor to know she'd taken time out of work to give in to one of her son's whims. Lila already worried that the job was too much for Stacy.

She couldn't afford to give the governor evidence to support that concern.

"Starting tomorrow, everyone gets ID badges. You need to wear these at all times when on the grounds."

Soft grumbles filled the room.

"It was my idea." Lila spoke up for the first time since Harlan convened the meeting. The grumbles subsided.

"There's a checkpoint outside this office now. As each of you leave, you'll sign out. This will be required at each checkpoint—sign in and sign out."

And the situation just kept getting worse, Stacy thought. Maybe she could talk a checkpoint guard into keeping her trip to the stable and back to himself, but she couldn't ask him to let her go through without signing in or out.

Which left her with only one choice.

She'd have to bypass security and sneak her way to the stable to pick up her son.

"I THINK THEY TOOK IT WELL, considering," Lila commented to Harlan after the employees filed out of her office.

"I suppose I should have softened the blow a little more," he admitted. "But we really should have put these protocols into place the day you returned from Austin."

The governor leaned back in her chair, crossing one leg over the other. She looked tired and tense, though she'd hidden her distress quite well while the rest of her staff had been in the room with her. "Austin police haven't found any leads. They're studying the surveillance systems at the capitol, but they haven't found anything yet."

"Have you ever considered that it might have been an inside job?" Harlan asked.

Lila met his gaze. "I've considered it. I don't want to."

"From what I understand, your decision to make the announcement of your candidacy was pretty last-minute."

"Yes. I've been considering a run for a while, but the decision to hold the press conference was spur of the moment. The only person I told more than two days beforehand was Stacy."

Harlan felt a funny dipping sensation in his gut. "An outside agitator wouldn't have had much of a chance to figure out a way inside your defenses in such a short amount of time."

"You're not suggesting Stacy—"

"I'm not suggesting anything," he said quickly. "I'm just asking questions, trying to get a clearer picture of the flow of information around here."

"We've always run things here at the ranch differently than we do when we're at the capitol," Lila admitted. "This is my home. The people who work here are like family to me. We treat each other that way."

"That's a nice way to do business if you can," Harlan conceded. "But you're going to have to start doing things differently, especially now that you're seeking higher office."

Lila sighed, closing her eyes. "I know."

"It'll only get worse if you're successful in your bid."

Her lips curved. "I know that, too. I've always considered it a fair trade." She opened her eyes again, pinning him with her strong blue-eyed gaze. "I'd just hoped to put off that moment for a little longer."

"I'll try to make it as comfortable for you and your staff as I can. Within limits."

Lila cocked her head. "Bart told me you were the perfect person to head my security team for this fundraiser. He said you're completely unsentimental and unafraid to be brutally honest. I need you to be that for me."

"I'll try to always be straight with you."

"I know. I just hope you won't forget what I said about my staff being like family."

"I won't, ma'am. I promise."

"Go see how your protocols are working." Lila smiled at him. "I can see you're curious."

He was, a little. He suspected it would take a little while for people to get used to such strict control of their movements after being given the run of the place for so long.

He hated having to do it to them; as much as he'd thrived under the discipline of the Marine Corps, he had fond memories of his youth in the North Georgia mountains, where the hot summer days had seemed the purest form of freedom—hours of tramping through the woods and playing with friends without school bells or homework to interrupt the fun. His parents had both worked, leaving him in the half-interested care of his teenage sister, whose only rules were to stay out of the hospital and stay out of jail. Somehow, he'd managed to keep those rules, though sometimes by the finest of hairs.

He checked with the guard outside the governor's office. All fifteen staffers had signed the sheet. His gaze slid down to the clean, bold signature of Stacy Giordano.

She'd seemed restless during the meeting. And when he'd laid out the details of the security protocols, she'd looked frustrated and unhappy.

The only person I told more than two days beforehand was Stacy. The governor's words rang in his head.

The idea that she could have anything to do with the threat against the governor seemed ludicrous on its face. She'd been the one who found the bomb. She'd dashed right into the debris, stayed there even after she found the bomb and any reasonable person would have completely understood if she'd decided to clear out and let the bomb squad figure a way in to the bomb.

Of course, if she'd been the bomber, or knew the bomber, she'd feel pretty confident the explosive device wasn't going to blow. Not while she was in the line of fire, anyway.

Pulling his phone from his pocket, he jotted a note to do a background check on the governor's office staff. He should have started this yesterday, when he found out he was going to be in charge of security for the upcoming fundraiser. He'd already begun to suspect the bombing could have been an inside job.

Do you really think it's Stacy Giordano?

He had learned to trust his instincts, and something about Stacy's demeanor during the meeting had set off his radar, big-time. She didn't like the security protocols one bit, and he wanted to know why.

He jotted another note on his phone.

Check Stacy Giordano first.

TOMORROW, STACY PROMISED herself, *I'll stick to the security protocols like glue.* Just not today, when her five-year-old was probably counting the minutes she was late and working himself up into a fine lather.

The security checkpoint was stationed about seventy yards up the dirt road that led to the stable, but she decided she could stay out of sight for most of the trip to the horse barn by circling around and approaching from the rear, through a rough bit of scrubby pasture fenced off to keep the horses away from the treacherous minefield of gopher holes. Reclaiming the fallow land was on the ranch agenda for next spring, but for now, it gave Stacy a more stealthy approach to the stable.

From inside the horse barn, she heard the familiar sounds of a working stable—the soft nickers of horses and the murmur of conversations between the grooms working inside. Over the other sounds, she heard the high-pitched sound of her son's voice responding to something a groom had said. She smiled at the sweet, familiar sound.

"Forget something?"

The gravelly drawl, close to her ear, nearly made her jump out of her skin. Whirling, she found herself face-to-face with Harlan McClain, who stood only inches away, his brown eyes hard with suspicion.

"You scared the life out of me." She pressed her hand to her chest, her cheeks hot with guilt.

His only response was a slow, thorough appraisal of her, head to foot and back again, as if he were trying to see right through to her bones.

"Do you need something from me?" she asked when the continuing silence grew excruciating.

"The truth would be a good start."

"The truth?" she echoed, not yet ready to incriminate herself, just in case he didn't realize she'd sneaked her way here instead of following the protocols he'd set up.

"The road from the governor's house to here is straight and remarkably level for a dirt road. Very easy walking."

She didn't reply, although she knew where he was headed.

"So I have to wonder why you chose to walk a quarter mile farther than necessary through a scrubby field to get here when you had such a nice easy path."

His caustic tone made her bristle, driving away her lingering sense of chagrin. "Are you accusing me of something, Mr. McClain?"

"You bypassed the security checkpoint. Deliberately. I'd like to know why."

She pressed her lips into a flat line, growing angry. "Is this how it's going to be from now on? One step outside your rules and it's the third degree?" She knew some of her anger was fueled by her dismay at being caught breaking the rules, but not all of it. The Harlan McClain standing in front of her seemed a completely different man than the Southern gentleman who'd treated her with such kind concern the day of the bombing. His eyes had been warm and comforting then, not hard and cold like stone as they were now.

He shifted so that he blocked out the afternoon sun, plunging his face into shadow until she could no longer see his expression. But the tense set of his muscles as he towered over her was enough to convey his hostile attitude. "Someone tried to kill your boss two days ago. I would think you of all people would understand why I asked y'all to keep to the security protocols. So you mind telling me why you didn't?"

She couldn't stand not being able to read his expression, so she took a couple of steps to the side, trying to force him to turn so the glare of the sun no longer backlit his face.

His hand snaked out and snagged her arm, making her gasp. He loosened his grip at the sound but didn't let go. "Where do you think you're going?"

"Mommy, you're late."

She whipped her head around to find her son standing a few feet away, looking up at her with a disapproving gleam in his blue eyes.

"I know, baby. I'm sorry. I had a meeting and I couldn't get away as early as I'd hoped."

"Couldn't you tell them you had to come here?" Zachary asked.

Stacy shot a quick look at Harlan. He looked confused.

"Who are you?" Zachary asked bluntly, his gaze following Stacy's to settle on Harlan McClain.

Harlan cleared his throat and dropped Stacy's arm. "I'm Harlan McClain. Who are you?"

"Zachary Giordano," he answered formally, as he was prone to do. It had taken Stacy a while to get used to his way of speaking. It was another symptom of his Asperger's syndrome, one that could be deceiving to people who didn't know his situation. Because he conversed so much more maturely than his peers, and was such a sponge when it came to learning the new things he wanted to learn, people often assumed he was just a very precocious child. Which he was, in many ways.

It was the ways in which he differed from other children that would keep his life from ever being considered normal.

"Zachary's my son."

Harlan nodded. "I guessed as much."

"He loves to ride," she added, "but we missed his Tuesday lesson because of…what happened in Austin."

"I see. So you thought you'd make it up to him?" Harlan glanced at Zachary, who was gazing up at him with an almost comical look of interest.

Seeing the signs of trouble on the horizon, Stacy quickly stepped between Harlan and Zachary. "Zachary, it's time to go back home now. I've got to get you cleaned up and ready for dinner." She turned to look at Harlan. "I'm sorry I broke protocol. I didn't want the governor to think I can't handle motherhood and the job at the same time."

Harlan's eyes narrowed. "You didn't want to sign the check-in list."

"Yes."

"Mommy, can Harlan come to dinner?"

"Mr. McClain," she corrected automatically, before she registered what he'd asked.

"Can Mr. McClain come to dinner?"

She looked at Harlan, warning him with her eyes to make a quick excuse. Zachary might have all the socialization difficulties that came with Asperger's, but that didn't mean he didn't form attachments to people. On the contrary, her son was prone to crushes on people. He latched on to friends at school, had a huge preference for one—but not both—of Lindsay Kemp's twin daughters, and just last week, he'd fallen instantly in love with the courier who dropped by the governor's office to leave some legal papers.

Once he was smitten, Zachary could be a full-bore pest, unable to read the signals people gave him that he was coming on entirely too strong. And right now, Zachary was showing all the signs of an impending crush. "Zachary, I'm sure Mr. McClain has something else to do—"

"Actually, dinner sounds good," Harlan interjected. "What time should I be there?"

She stared at him, disbelieving. Talk about not reading people's silent cues... "I really don't have anything in the house to cook."

"You have bread and cheese? A grilled cheese sandwich sounds fine."

She looked at him with narrowed eyes, not buying it. For one thing, a man his size would never be fine with a grilled cheese sandwich unless it was wrapped around a steak. And for another, she could tell he was still suspicious of her decision to bypass the checkpoint, despite her explanation. "Mr. McClain—"

"I think we've gotten off on the wrong foot here, Ms. Giordano, and considering we have to work together for the next little while, we probably shouldn't let that continue. Don't you agree?" His voice softened, his drawl coming out to play a little more. "I'm not going to tell the governor about this. I reckon you've got to do whatever you can to keep all those balls you're juggling in the air."

Relief rippled through her. "Thank you."

"I do need to go over a few things with you—get a copy of the guest list you're working up so we can vet everyone. I'll also need to know your plans for the physical layout— what rooms you're going to use, where we can set up security."

"Of course."

"I'd just as soon get that started tonight rather than waiting for later—we shouldn't have taken today off."

She hadn't taken the day off, but she wasn't about to point out that fact to him. "So you're serious about dinner?"

"Yeah, but I was sort of lying about grilled cheese being okay. Why don't I pick up something at Talk of the Town? I work with the owner's fiancé—maybe I can get a deal." He grinned.

"Mr. McClain, did you know that quarter horses are called that because they were bred for running quarter-mile races?" Zachary asked.

"I did," Harlan answered, turning to smile at Zachary.

Zachary grinned back, making Stacy's heart contract. "I knew you would."

"Why's that?"

"Because you're wearing a horse."

Harlan looked down at the logo on the left breast of his golf shirt. "Well, what do you know. I am."

"Did you know that quarter horses were first called quarter-mile horses?" Zachary asked.

"Now, that I didn't know."

"I have a book. You can borrow it." Zachary moved closer, gazing up at Harlan with a look Stacy was coming to recognize as trouble waiting to happen. He was definitely developing a crush on Harlan McClain.

And that was bound to be nothing but trouble for Stacy.

"Thanks, Zachary. I might take you up on that." Harlan turned to Stacy. "Is seven okay for dinner?"

Now was her chance to back out, she thought. But he'd more or less suggested the dinner would be a business meeting, too, so she could hardly say no, could she?

She swallowed a sigh, overwhelmed with the growing certainty that she was racing headlong into one big mess. "Sure. Seven is fine."

She grabbed Zachary's hand and started walking down the road toward the checkpoint. Harlan caught up with them. "I'll get you through the checkpoint without having to sign out."

She flashed a grateful smile, but inside, her stomach was turning flips, especially when his hand brushed her back as he guided her toward the checkpoint.

Maybe Zachary wasn't the only one forming a crush.

Chapter Six

"He really likes horses, huh?" Harlan asked Stacy, watching Zachary pretend to feed pieces of apple to the toy horses sitting next to him at the kitchen table.

"He's single-minded about subjects that interest him." She spoke carefully when discussing her son, Harlan noticed. That caution probably explained her stealth this afternoon at the stables. Though she was clearly a good mom—Zachary was as smart as a whip and relatively well-behaved—she seemed determined to act, on the job at least, as if she weren't a mother at all.

He had served with women in Iraq, mothers who'd been forced to leave their kids home with family or their husbands while they served their country in a war zone, never sure they'd make it back alive. He understood the pressures women were under when the demands of their jobs clashed with the interests of their families. Nobody really won in that kind of situation.

"I've made just about all the calls I needed to make, and I'm going to ask the ad agency to do a rush job on getting the invitations to our donor list set up and ready to go by Friday," Stacy said to fill the silence that had fallen between them. "They'll drop Friday and most should be in home by Wednesday or Thursday, which means they'll have a little over a week to get back to us with their RSVPs."

"That sounds good." He wasn't really worried about the vagaries of direct mail. He was more interested in whether or not she agreed with his solidifying belief that the bomb at the capitol was an inside job. "Stacy, has the governor hired anyone new in the last few weeks?"

Her eyebrows lifted at the question. "Not in the office staff. I'm not sure about the ranch hands—they come and go more regularly than the political staff do, and I don't have anything to do with the hiring, so I wouldn't know."

"The ranch staff wouldn't know much about the governor's comings and goings, would they?"

"Not day to day, no."

"But they know about some of the comings and goings?"

"Well, sure," she said. "If the governor's having people to visit, they'll know. If she's going to be away from the ranch overnight, some of them, at least, would know."

"Harlan, will you go riding with me?" Zachary asked, looking up at Harlan with curious blue eyes.

Stacy glanced at Harlan. "Mr. McClain," she gently corrected. "And Mr. McClain is going to be really busy for a while. In fact, I'm going to be busy, too. But I promise we'll make up the riding lessons if we miss any. Okay?"

Zachary's dark brows met in the middle. "We can't miss any riding lessons, Mommy. The horses depend on seeing me."

She laughed softly, though she darted another quick look at Harlan. "I'm sure they will have plenty of people to keep them entertained until you can get back to them. But in the meantime, I have a job I have to do, and I need you to be a big boy and help me out. Can you do that?"

"Help you out how?"

"Just by being a sweet boy and understanding that sometimes, you'll have to play by yourself while I'm working."

Zachary fell silent again.

"Must be hard keeping up with him and your job at the same time," Harlan murmured.

Stacy's dark eyebrows met in a V, as Zachary's had. "I manage," she said shortly.

Great. He'd said the wrong thing again.

Zachary broke the tense silence. "Can you get me another book about horses, Mommy? I've read the one I have five times."

Stacy released a soft breath. "I can get you another book on horses, Zachary. But maybe you should try reading one of the other books I bought you for your birthday first. How about the book about trains?"

"But I want to read about horses."

The kid was single-minded, Harlan thought. "Locomotive trains were once called iron horses," he told the little boy. "Did you know that?"

Zachary looked skeptical. "Trains don't eat apples. And they don't have manes. And horses don't have engines."

"I think it's because trains took the place of horses for travel back in the days before cars and trucks and airplanes." Stacy smiled, but Harlan saw a hint of sadness behind the smile, as if the conversation was causing her pain. "And since locomotives were made of iron, they called them iron horses."

"Why didn't they just call them trains?" Zachary asked.

"I'm sure they did that, too," Harlan interjected. "It was like a nickname. You know what a nickname is, don't you?"

"Miss Charlotte at school calls the girl who sits next to me Patricia, but we all call her Patty. She says it's her nickname. I think Miss Charlotte should call her Patty, too, if that's what she wants to be called. Don't you?"

Harlan looked up at Stacy. "How old is he?"

"Five." She gave him a look that seemed almost wary before she added, "And a half."

"He's very bright. You must spend a lot of time reading to him." Harlan ventured a smile, a little taken aback at how nervous she seemed with him now. Just a few days earlier, in Austin, she'd seemed confident and strong, nothing like the woman on edge facing him now.

"I can read," Zachary piped up. "I read the book about horses all by myself."

Harlan looked at Stacy for confirmation. She gave a slight nod and tried a smile back at him, but it looked forced.

"How's that hamburger, Zachary?" he asked her son, noticing that the boy had barely touched his food.

"It has mustard," Zachary said bluntly. "I hate mustard."

"I'm sorry—he tends to say what he thinks without worrying how it sounds." Stacy reached across the table for the hamburger. "Zachary, you could have told me it had mustard on it. I would have scraped it off for you."

"It gets all in the bread. It never stops tasting like mustard," the boy said flatly. "Can I have a cookie now?"

Stacy frowned. "Let me open you some soup first. You know you have to eat dinner before you eat dessert."

"I'm sorry," Harlan asked, feeling like an idiot. "I should have thought to ask what he'd want on it."

"It's okay," Stacy assured him quickly, digging in her cabinet for a can of soup. "If you don't have children, you don't know to anticipate things like that."

"I'll have to make a Zachary list, then." Harlan grinned at the boy, who looked back at him with a blank-looking stare. "Likes horses, knows how to read, doesn't like mustard."

"I also like cookies," Zachary added.

"Noted."

Stacy was in the middle of heating the bowl of soup in the microwave when her cell phone rang. She looked at the display and frowned. "It's Greg Merritt. I'll have to get this."

She moved into the living room, seeking privacy, but

the guesthouse was too small to afford her much. From her end of the conversation, it sounded as if the governor's campaign manager wanted an instant update on the invitation list Stacy had been working on.

The microwave oven beeped, signaling it was finished cooking Zachary's soup. Neither Stacy nor Zachary seemed to notice.

Harlan got up and retrieved the soup from the microwave oven, snagging the spoon Stacy had left on the counter on the way back to the table. He set the soup in front of Zachary. "Mmm, chicken and noodles. I used to love that when I was a kid."

Zachary picked up his spoon. "Why don't you love it now?"

"Well, I suppose I'd still love it now. I just don't eat a lot of soup anymore."

"But if you loved it before and you love it now, why don't you eat it anymore?" Zachary's forehead furrowed, making him look like a confused cherub.

"I eat other things."

"Horses eat carrots as well as apples." Zachary turned his attention back to the toy horse. "Do you have a horse?"

"I live in a small apartment, so I can't have a horse there. If I lived somewhere else, maybe I would." His family had been too poor to own horses when he was a kid, but he had learned to ride thanks to a schoolmate whose family owned a stable with several Tennessee walking horses.

Across the room, Stacy's voice rose. "Greg, I can't get a whole new group of names added to the list before tomorrow morning. You're just going to have to reschedule."

"Mommy, we don't live in a small apartment. Can we have a horse?" Zachary slipped down from his chair and crossed to Stacy, tugging at her blouse. "Mommy, we can have a horse because we don't live in a small apartment."

Stacy made a shushing sound, stroking her son's head. "Yes, I know we're under the gun—"

"Mommy, we can have a horse! Harlan said so!"

Stacy shot Harlan a questioning look.

Harlan hurried over, gently steering Zachary back to the table. "Zachary, let's go back and eat your soup."

"You can have it," Zachary said dismissively, wriggling out of Harlan's grasp and returning to his mother. "Mommy, can we go get our horse now?"

"Zachary, your mama's on the phone. Come back and eat your soup," Harlan said, keeping his voice as low as possible.

Zachary ignored him. "Mommy—"

Stacy put her hand over the phone receiver. "Just a second, Zachary— Yes, Greg, I'm still listening to you—"

Harlan reached down and picked Zachary up, carrying him toward the kitchen. Immediately, he realized he'd done exactly the wrong thing. Zachary started struggling as if Harlan were trying to abduct him, his hands flapping wildly and his head rolling. Stacy shot Harlan a look of sheer disbelief.

Well, hell, Harlan thought, feeling about as stupid as he ever had. But might as well make the most of his screwup. He carried Zachary into the kitchen and planted him on the chair in front of his bowl of soup.

"Mommy!" Zachary wailed. He kept flapping his hands frantically.

Harlan gently caught the boy's hands to hold them still. "I'm sorry I scared you, but you need to let your mama finish her business. Can't you wait until she's done?"

Zachary went silent, staring at Harlan with blue eyes full of accusation. "You touched me."

Harlan dropped his hands away. "I know. I'm sorry."

"Mommy says l should never let someone else touch me. Only Mommy. I'm telling."

Oh, great. Now the kid thought he was some sort of pervert. "I think your mama already knows. And I'm sorry, Zachary. Your mama's right—you shouldn't let any-body touch you but her without your permission. But your mama—"

"Can take care of my own son without your interference," Stacy finished for him.

He turned his head to find her only a couple of feet away, her hands on her hips. Her dark eyes blazed at him.

He held up his hands in surrender. "I know. I'm sorry. It's just—I see a situation developing, I try to fix it. But I had no right."

"No. You didn't."

"I can see it was a mistake to try to meet for dinner," Harlan looked down at Zachary, who had apparently gotten over the trauma of being picked up and hauled to the table. He was eating his soup again, one hand closed over a toy horse, making it trot circles around his bowl.

"I think so, too."

Her short, angry replies were beginning to bring out a little of his own ire. What crime had he committed to deserve Stacy Giordano's cold fury? Picking up her kid? He didn't hurt Zachary, and the kid was acting like a brat, anyway. Maybe if she spent a little more time with him...

"I'll check in with you in the morning. We have a lot to go over," he said brusquely, crossing to the closet where she'd hung his coat.

She caught up with him. "I'll do whatever you ask me to do to make this fundraiser happen safely. But keep your hands off my son."

His control snapped. "What the hell is your problem? I

didn't hurt your kid. I was trying to insert a little discipline into a situation that was getting completely out of control—"

"It's not your place to discipline my son."

"I just tried to get him to be quiet so you could do your job," Harlan threw back at her. "The kid could talk paint off a wall, and he has no sense of control over his impulses. Do you let him just do whatever he wants whenever he wants?"

"He has impulse control issues because he has Asperger's syndrome," Stacy snapped back. "Ever heard of it?"

Harlan shook his head.

Stacy shoved his coat at him. "Look it up. And if you can't deal with what you find, stay far away from my son."

He stepped out into the cool October evening, wincing at the sound of the door shutting firmly behind him the second he stepped through the opening.

"That went well, don't you think?" he asked the waxing moon rising over the cottonwood trees to the east.

The moon remained silent.

He glanced at his watch. Just a little after seven-thirty. And he'd barely touched his burger.

Yeah, a spectacularly successful night all the way around.

Maybe he could coax the cook at the ranch house to make him a sandwich. He could eat it in the office the governor had set up for him down the hall from her own.

Anything was preferable to going to his lonely, sparsely furnished apartment and trying to pretend it felt like home.

Or that he didn't feel like a complete idiot.

"ARE WE GOING to get a horse?" Zachary asked.

Stacy's head was pounding, but she tried not to let her son see how much stress she was feeling. "Zachary, we don't actually own this house. Ms. Lila just lets us live here, so we can't bring a horse onto her property. She has her own horses and you get to ride them sometimes, don't you?"

"Only sometimes," Zachary complained. "I want a horse I can ride all the time. And I can feed it apples and carrots and give it a name I pick. I think I would name him Zachary's Horse. Because he'd be mine. And a horse."

Stacy let out a soft chuckle, feeling a bit of her tension beginning to ease away. "Zachary, we're going to be staying here with the governor for a long while more." At least, she hoped they were, although if Harlan McClain was the vindictive sort, he could be making trouble for her even as they spoke.

She pushed the bleak thought aside. "We're just going to have to ride Ms. Lila's horses for now. If we ever get our own place, though, and we have enough room and it's not against the law, we'll talk about getting our own horse. I promise."

Zachary looked as if he were inclined to argue some more, but Stacy couldn't spend the rest of her evening treading the same rhetorical ground with her son when her job might be dangling by a very thin thread.

"Zachary, would you like to go see Chico?" she asked, taking her son by the hand. Chico was the half-Siamese cat that belonged to the governor's groundskeeper, Miguel. The cat seemed to disdain most visitors, but for some reason, he loved Stacy's young son.

They walked along the dark path to the original ranch house, where the ranch staff now worked, and dutifully checked in with the guard at the checkpoint. Miguel and his wife, Rhonda, greeted her and Zachary with delight, and almost immediately, Chico wound himself around Zachary's ankles, purring audibly.

"Rhonda, I'm so sorry to ask this of you, but can you keep an eye on Zachary for a few minutes? I need to speak to the governor for a little while."

"Of course, we'll watch him," Rhonda said immediately,

smiling her understanding. Rhonda and Miguel had become her immediate allies here on the ranch, as they had a grandson with autism and understood the challenges their own daughter and son-in-law were now facing.

Stacy was very lucky to be surrounded with so many people who were willing and eager to help her out with her son. She just had to make sure she still had this job come morning.

As she walked back to the main house, she spotted Harlan McClain's shiny black truck parked in the side parking area, near the governor's office and the smaller office the governor had set up for him earlier that day.

So he'd gone from her house straight to see the governor. That couldn't be good.

Tamping down her dread, she signed in with the man standing guard at the side entrance and entered, heading straight to the governor's office. She expected to find her deep in discussion with Harlan, but to her surprise, the governor was alone.

"I'm surprised to see you here so late, Stacy." Lila slipped her glasses off and waved at the empty chair in front of her desk. "Have you hit a snag with the fundraiser?"

"No, I— No. Everything's going surprisingly well. I was able to reach more people on the first call than I expected."

"Perhaps my recent brush with death has made people feel more inclined to take your calls," Lila said with a wry smile. "In case it's their last chance to do business with me."

"Don't even joke about that," Stacy said, her stomach aching with the memory of just how close they'd both come to dying only a couple of days earlier.

"Sorry. Sometimes the only way to deal with a bad memory is to laugh at it." Lila leaned back in her chair. "So, if you're not here with a work problem, it must be something personal. Is your ex giving you trouble?"

"No, I haven't heard from Anthony in a couple of months." Stacy started to get up, realizing she'd made a mistake coming here. She wanted to hide her troubles from the governor, not lay them at the woman's feet.

"Sit. Spill."

Stacy resumed her seat. Before she knew it, she'd told the governor everything about her disastrous reaction to Harlan McClain's attempt to discipline her son. "I know he meant well, but I didn't take it well. You know how defensive I can be when it comes to Zachary—"

"And you thought he'd come here and tell on you?"

Stacy nodded. "I guess that was stupid, huh?"

"Not stupid, but I have to tell you, if you were worried that I'd sack you just because some big strappin' hunk of a fellow came in here telling tales, you don't know me very well. A man who'd tattle like a grade-schooler about something so petty isn't the sort of man I'd want guarding my rose garden, much less my life."

Stacy smiled. "So he hasn't even spoken to you tonight?"

"He dropped by a few minutes ago to make sure it was okay for him to stay late and do a little work. He didn't mention seeing you."

Stacy felt a sliver of guilt dig into the center of her chest. Here she'd been expecting the worst from him, and he hadn't even mentioned seeing her at all, much less spilled all her deep, dark secrets. "I guess I'd better go apologize for snapping at him."

"Might be a good idea," Lila agreed. "You know where to find him."

Stacy left the governor's office and walked down the long hallway, past her own office, to the office she and the governor had helped set up earlier that morning. The door was open a few inches, but Stacy knocked anyway. "Mr. McClain?"

He looked up as she entered, his expression wary. He filled the small office, not just with his muscular chest and broad shoulders but also the intensity of personality burning in his dark eyes.

He gave her a brief, businesslike nod. "Ms. Giordano."

"Mr. McClain." She paused where she stood a few feet away from him, trying to figure out what to say next. She could explain herself a little more directly, tell him why her salary was so important, how it paid for the therapies that gave her son half a chance at a more normal life. She could tell him how she hadn't anticipated being left alone to deal with her son's problems without his father's help.

But when she opened her mouth to speak, only one word came out. "Sorry," she said.

And realized he'd just said the exact same thing.

Chapter Seven

She looked tired, Harlan thought. Not just tired like a woman who'd had a long day but tired like a woman who'd had a long and stressful life. And he was more than a little surprised when the first words out of her mouth were an apology.

"Nothing to be sorry for." Rising from his desk chair, Harlan waved at the armless chair in front of his desk that was, temporarily at least, the only other seating accommodation he could offer. "Where's Zachary?"

"I took him to visit Miguel and Rhonda—Miguel's the groundskeeper."

"I've met him. Nice guy."

"Their youngest grandson is autistic."

Heat burned Harlan's neck. "Sorry about what happened with Zachary. I looked up Asperger's syndrome, like you suggested."

"I overreacted. I'm just a mama bear where my son's concerned. I should have explained instead of getting angry. It's just—he's going to have problems ahead of him, no matter what I do. Therapy only goes so far." She hunched forward as if the world was heavy on her back. "Sooner or later, kids will start making fun of him because he's different. He's not going to have any kind of defense against it. And it's worse for him because it's not immediately obvious he has a problem."

"He has an amazing vocabulary for his age. I understand that's a symptom?"

"Or a blessing," she said with a sad half smile that made Harlan's chest hurt. "I'm luckier than a lot of mothers with special needs children. My son talks to me. He communicates pretty well. If he's in the mood, he'll hug me."

"But he doesn't respond to most of your overtures, right?"

"Reading social cues is beyond him. He doesn't know that when I frown at him when he's making a pest of himself, it means he should stop. He doesn't understand that not everybody loves horses as much as he does."

"How long has he been obsessed with horses?"

"Since his first rocking horse. When I took him for riding lessons, that was that. It's all he talks about these days." Her smile was wider this time, less bittersweet. "When he was three, he was obsessed with his father's cell phone. He'd sneak it out of Anthony's briefcase and play with it. He made God knows how many calls to people on Anthony's list of contacts." Her smile faded. "Anthony got so angry. He thought Zachary was acting up and that if he disciplined him, he'd behave."

Harlan's heart sank. "And when you saw me pick him up and try to make him stop bothering you—"

She nodded. "Anthony didn't know, either. Not then."

"He must have felt bad about how he behaved once you figured out something was different about Zachary." Harlan had felt like a complete lowlife, himself. He couldn't imagine how the boy's father must have reacted.

"He felt bad that he had a defective son." The bitterness in her voice came as a bit of a surprise. "He didn't stick around long after that."

Harlan frowned. "He just left?"

Stacy's cheeks went pink. She stood up, already turning toward the door. "I didn't come here to talk about my marriage. I just wanted to say I was sorry and I hope we can work together without letting what happened tonight get in the way."

He rose with her. "We can do that. How about we start fresh in the morning? Eight o'clock?"

"Eight it is." She managed another tentative smile. "I'd better go get Zachary before he makes Miguel and Rhonda regret they said they'd watch him."

Harlan walked her to the door of his office. "Be careful going back to your house."

She shot him a wry look. "This place is crawling with security. I've never been safer in my life."

Watching her walk down the hall toward the exit, he fervently hoped she was right. But he wasn't sure anyone on the ranch was safe at the moment, no matter how many checkpoints he'd set up. For earlier that day, before he met Stacy for dinner, he'd gone over the security summaries from the event at the capitol, and something had struck him as highly significant.

Nobody on the staff at the capitol had known what the governor had planned until the evening before it happened. They'd worked overnight to set up the dais and the sound system for the announcement. To get the event set up on time, the governor had to send her own staffers from the ranch—both office staff and ranch staff—to aid with the setup.

About the only way the bomber could have known to set the bomb when and where he did was if he'd had prior notice. Which meant the culprit almost certainly was a member of the governor's staff, which had known about the event at least a day and a half before the staff at the

capitol. Whoever had planted the bombs had to be part of
the governor's staff in Freedom.

And that put Stacy and her son right in the crosshairs.

"YOU CAN'T BE SERIOUS." Stacy stared at Harlan with a mix-
ture of disbelief and growing horror the next morning, when
they met for their first orientation meeting. "Why on earth
would anyone here want to hurt Lila?"

"Maybe she said the wrong thing to the wrong person."
Harlan shrugged. "People go off for all kinds of reasons."

"Not this staff," Stacy disagreed. "People here would
open a vein for Lila. She's the kind of honest, straightfor-
ward and sensible person this nation needs, and we'd never
do anything to sabotage her, much less hurt her."

"And she pays well."

Heat rose in Stacy's face. "That's not the reason I took
this job. I've been following the governor's career since I
was a teenager in Arkansas. I knew even then she was going
to be big news. That's the way almost all of us who work for
her feel. I don't know how much you know about working
in politics, but it's not the kind of job you do just because
you want to bring home a nice paycheck."

"Fair enough," Harlan conceded, looking pleased with
her answer. "But what about the ranch staff? Could it have
been one of them?"

"Lila doesn't exactly include them in her event planning,"
Stacy pointed out.

But she didn't exactly treat them as potential leaks, either,
Stacy had to admit. She'd warned the governor more than
once that she should be a little more discreet about talking
government business in the stables, at least. Stacy would
concede that the house staff were loyal employees whom
the governor treated like beloved family. But only the most
senior of ranch hands were long-timers. Most of the junior

stable grooms and a lot of the cowboys were relatively recent hires, as the jobs could be dirty, grueling and physically demanding. There was a lot of turnover.

"What is it?" Harlan's eyes narrowed. Apparently he'd noticed her hesitation.

"The governor spends a lot of time out of her office when she's here. She loves this ranch, and she likes to be hands-on about how it's run when she gets the chance."

"And it's possible she might have said something about the announcement event in Austin within the hearing of one of the ranch hands?"

"Maybe. You'll have to ask the governor if she said anything to anyone about the event within earshot of the ranch staff. I don't remember any particular incident, but she tries to oversee ranch business three or four times a week when she's here in Freedom, so there could have been ample opportunity."

"I'll definitely ask her." Harlan nodded. "Meanwhile, when you get a chance in between your phone calls, will you get me a list of the ranch hands? The governor only gave me names of the office staff for my background checks, but I reckon now I need to go a little deeper."

"You're doing background checks?" Stacy blurted, then realized it was a stupid question. Of course he was doing background checks. It would be a foolish breach of security protocol not to. "I just mean—we were all screened before we took jobs with the governor."

"I know, but those screeners were looking for different things than I am. And they didn't know what I know now."

"That you think one of us could be a bomber?"

He flashed her a wry smile. "It does add a new wrinkle."

Stacy dragged her gaze away from the dimple that had formed in Harlan's cheek when he smiled and made a note on her BlackBerry to get the list of ranch staff for Harlan.

"I'll also want to see your event plans each step of the way," Harlan added.

She looked up in surprise. "By each step, do you mean—"

"I mean I want to know everything you've done each day toward throwing this shindig. Is that a problem?"

She frowned. "It's a little control-freakish," she blurted before she could stop herself.

Harlan's lips curved again. "Maybe. But if I find security loopholes at this stage, it'll be a lot easier to fix them than if we wait until the party's half-planned, right?"

She couldn't quibble with that. "I work from home in the afternoons, unless Zachary has a riding lesson. Then I work from wherever I am. But I can check back in near the end of the day." Her mind was already racing to figure out what she could do with Zachary during the time she was supposed to be meeting with Harlan. Charlotte, Zachary's preschool special ed teacher, was often happy to help out, but Stacy would never ask her to babysit every afternoon.

"You know you can bring Zachary here if you need to," Harlan said quietly.

She looked up and found him watching her with a look of sympathy that made her feel like a helpless idiot. "That's kind of you, but—"

"But you'd rather scramble around every day finding someone to watch him?"

She pressed her lips into a flat line. "I don't want you to accommodate me. I don't need special favors."

"You need to give yourself a break," Harlan said flatly. "And if it matters, I need you working at full attention, and you won't be doing that if you're worrying about your son."

"I suppose that's your way of saying you don't think I can do both? Work this job and be a mother to my son?"

Harlan shot her a frowning look. "I don't talk in riddles. I say what I mean."

"I'm sorry," she said. "And thank you."

His frown faded. "I need to check in with some of my associates, so go ahead and make the calls you need to make this morning, and we can regroup after you pick up your son from school. What time will that be?"

"I pick him up around noon. I usually get him fed and settled down and then go back to work."

"Perfect. We'll regroup after lunch." He gave a nod that she took as a dismissal. With a tiny sigh, she headed out of Harlan's office and returned to her own, where a long to-do list taunted her from her desk blotter.

Nine in the morning and her head was already starting to pound from the stress. How long was she going to be able to keep juggling her job and her son's overwhelming needs?

And what would be left of her by the end?

LILA LOCKHART DROPPED BY Harlan's office around ten-thirty to check on how his first full day at work was going. "Is there anything more you need from me?"

Harlan smiled at the governor. "I think it's just a matter of getting everything done at this point. Thanks for the files on your staff. It helped to have access to what background checks had already been run."

"You didn't find any problems, did you?"

He shook his head. "No. You have good instincts about the people on your political staff. Do you also hire your ranch staff personally?"

"Not all of them. I hired the foreman, and the head groom, Cory, has been with my family for years. Why do you ask?"

"Stacy said you don't always restrict your political discussions to your office and the main house."

"That's true. I don't," the governor conceded. "Feel free to have Stacy round up a list of our ranch staff if you think they need to be investigated, as well. I'll warn them what's coming so they don't become alarmed."

"No, don't do that," Harlan said. "I don't want to tip off someone if he or she is behind the bombing."

He could tell she didn't like the idea of screening the ranch staff behind their backs, but she finally gave a reluctant nod. "Speaking of Stacy, how are you two getting along?"

"Fine," he said, wishing he believed the assurance himself. They'd started off well enough, thanks to the bombing, which had forced them to work together smoothly or else. But real life had blown that camaraderie to bits, and short of another crisis, he wasn't sure when they'd be on solid footing again.

Damned shame, really. She was the first woman he'd met in a long time who didn't remind him the least bit of his ex-wife. Alexis wanted nothing to do with kids, for one thing.

Like a fool, he'd thought she'd change her mind.

"Stacy's an interesting woman." Lila settled into the chair across from his desk. "Have you read her file?"

It had been the first he'd picked up. He'd told himself that, as Lila's most trusted aide, she was the biggest potential threat if she was a traitor. But that was total bunk.

He'd just wanted to know more about her. What made her tick. What made her vulnerable.

What made her smile.

"What her husband did to her and that sweet boy is unconscionable."

Harlan agreed. Maybe Stacy's husband had other reasons for walking out of the marriage, but that was no excuse to cut himself out of his son's life. Beyond the court-ordered child support he paid like clockwork, he'd had nothing to do with his son in over a year, if the background check on

Paula Graves   85

Stacy was to be believed. The assessor had made a note that Stacy merited close monitoring—not because there was any question about her integrity but because as a mother of a special needs child, she would be particularly susceptible to outside pressures.

In other words, someone might try to use her son against her in order to get to Lila.

It wasn't an unfounded suggestion. He thought it might be a damned good idea to keep a close eye on Stacy himself, even if his motives weren't strictly professional.

And now that they were working closely together, he'd have a built-in reason to do so.

"Who is Harlan and why does Zachary talk about him non-stop?" Charlotte asked Stacy when Zachary's kindergarten class let out at noon that day.

Stacy managed a rueful laugh. "I was hoping he'd be over that by now." She explained to Charlotte about Harlan McClain's visit the night before, including the way things had gotten out of hand after Harlan tried to correct Zachary. "I really thought Zachary would have forgotten all about him after that, but I guess he got over the scare and remembered how interesting he thought Mr. McClain was."

Charlotte walked with Stacy out to her car. "Is he? Interesting, I mean?"

"He's different," Stacy admitted carefully. "He's from Georgia, so he has that accent." The one that made her nerves quiver just a little every time she heard it. "He's a former Marine, so he's got that G.I. Joe thing going for him."

"Mmm," Charlotte said with a grin. "Married?"

She'd assumed not, since he'd invited himself to dinner and then spent the next hours after that working at the ranch house office, but what did she really know about him? "I don't know," she admitted. "Does it matter?"

"Well, let's see. Zachary's crazy about him, apparently, and you've been blushing since I brought up the name. So, yeah. It probably matters."

"We work together. That's all. You know why that's all." Of the people in town, only a handful knew the full story of her marriage breakup. Charlotte was one of them. She knew the way Anthony had let Stacy and Zachary down when they'd needed him most, and she knew that Stacy had no intention of ever letting a man do that to her or her child again.

It surprised her, a little, that she'd let as much slip to Harlan McClain as she had. There was just something about him that seemed trustworthy. Maybe that's why the governor had chosen him to keep her safe. If anyone could ferret out a person's deepest, darkest secrets...

"They're not all like that, you know," Charlotte said. "Sometimes the guy is the one who gets hurt. The guy who's the one left behind to raise a kid with problems."

Stacy gave her friend a questioning look. "Are we talking about someone specific?"

Charlotte chuckled. "The father of one of my students. Nice guy. His wife apparently never grew up, though. She had a bad habit of having three-martini lunches and driving buzzed with her kid in the car."

Stacy winced. "What happened?"

"Killed herself and a family of three in an accident about three years ago. Only her daughter survived the crash, and she was left with a brain injury that required years of therapy. I had her in my kindergarten class last year—she was a lot better by then, but she still has some issues. She's in first grade now, doing a lot better."

"Poor baby."

"Her dad was left to deal with her therapy and the lawsuit

filed by the survivors of the other family that was killed in the crash. It was terrible for him."

"Hey, you're talking about Jeff Appleton, aren't you?" Stacy realized. The deputy had done some moonlighting work for the governor's security detail from time to time. She'd heard stories about his legal problems and the fact that he had a six-year-old daughter with special needs. The governor had suggested she should let Zachary meet Jeff's daughter, but Stacy didn't think her son was really ready for playdates yet.

"Yes. Nice guy. He's under a lot of stress. Maybe you should get to know him. You have a lot in common."

Stacy looked at her friend through narrowed eyes. The suggestion had seemed almost rote, as if Charlotte felt it was the polite thing to do, even though Stacy got the sense that Charlotte didn't really want Stacy to see Jeff as a romantic possibility.

Did she have a crush on the deputy herself?

Before Stacy could pose that question, Charlotte's eyes widened. She caught Stacy by the arm. "Stacy, where's Zachary?"

Stacy looked down at her side, where she'd last seen her son. But he wasn't there.

She looked around, certain she'd see him nearby, perhaps running laps around the day care's front lawn. She'd drummed warnings about running off into his head since he was three, and he was usually very good about obeying that rule, since he had an older child's understanding of the reasons behind it.

But Zachary was nowhere in sight. Nor had he gotten into the car without her realizing it.

He was just gone.

Fear gathered into a hard knot in the center of her chest. "Did you see him go anywhere?"

"No!" Charlotte's look of rising terror amplified Stacy's own level of anxiety. "I thought he was right there with you!"

A cold chill washed over her body, spreading gooseflesh along her arms and legs. The world around her seemed to have upended in the span of seconds, leaving her breathless and dizzy in an alien landscape where nothing seemed familiar.

Where was Zachary?

Chapter Eight

A thousand terrifying scenarios rampaged through Stacy's mind as she tried to remember when she'd last seen her son. She'd gotten involved in the conversation with Charlotte almost immediately, but Zachary was always so good about sticking close to her, and she was generally attentive.

If he'd left her side without her noticing, he must have sneaked away. And Zachary didn't normally sneak.

"Zachary?" Charlotte called out, looking more and more scared.

"He wouldn't have left unless he saw something that interested him," Stacy told Charlotte. "Maybe he saw someone on horseback?"

"Or one of his friends he obsesses over?"

"Let's fan out." Stacy tamped down her paralyzing panic so she could function again. "He didn't have time to go far. We just have to find out where he went."

As Charlotte hurried down the street toward the bank, calling Zachary's name, Stacy went the opposite direction, her heart pounding like a timpani in her chest. A sense of disorientation lingered, but she forced aside the crimson veil of panic and reoriented herself as quickly as she could.

You're in Freedom, Texas. You know this place like the back of your hand by now. So does Zachary. So where would he go? What would interest him enough to make him sneak away?

She checked at Talk of the Town first. Zachary liked the diner as well as he liked any place in town. Faith and the other workers there knew about his condition and treated him well even when he was being a complete pest. Plus, if she put out the alert there, news of her missing son would be around town in minutes—even better than an Amber alert.

She'd barely set foot in the place when she heard a man's voice call her name. There was no missing the Georgia drawl or the deep timbre of his baritone voice. She looked up to find Harlan McClain sitting at a booth, waving her over. And across from him sat Zachary, reaching across the table to pluck a fry from Harlan's lunch plate.

"Lose something?" Harlan asked.

Relief overwhelmed Stacy, making her legs tremble. "Zachary, you scared me to death! Why did you wander off like that? You know we've talked about that!"

Zachary looked up at her as if she'd lost her mind. "I saw Harlan and I *had* to say hello."

"You had to, huh?" Stacy tried to calm down, not sure what she wanted to do more—hug her son or shake him for scaring the life out of her. She saw Harlan watching her with interest, as if trying to read her thoughts. "Sorry he bothered you."

"I'm sorry he scared you. But he's no bother. It's no fun eating alone." He shoved the squeeze bottle of ketchup toward Zachary, who grabbed it and squirted a ribbon of the sauce onto his purloined French fry.

"You should have called me the moment he came in." The scolding he deserved came out halfhearted, to her chagrin. They were just sort of heart-melting together, she thought, watching her son mimic Harlan's movements. Zachary could barely remember Anthony. A boy needed a father, and Zachary seemed determined to find one, on his own if necessary.

If she didn't know his heart would be broken when it ended, she might be inclined to encourage Zachary's new-found fascination with Harlan. Harlan McClain seemed lonely—another point against his being married—and he also seemed to genuinely appreciate her son, with all his quirks. God knew, she'd given him more than enough reason to back away from her and Zachary last night, hadn't she?

And yet, here he was, being kind to her son, letting him filch food right off his plate.

"I did try. You must have your phone off."

She pulled her phone from her purse and found that she'd put it on vibrate that morning during their meeting and had never switched it back to ring. "Sorry. I guess I was so freaked out I didn't feel it vibrating."

"You hungry?" Harlan asked her. "My food just got here. Y'all could join me."

"I'm hungry," Zachary said in a plaintive tone.

"Double-teaming me, are you?"

"We can make it a working lunch if you like," Harlan said. "I spent my morning going over that list of ranch staffers you compiled. Thought I'd pick your brain about a few of them."

The adrenaline that had driven her into the diner was leaking away as if someone had unplugged a drain. Her wobbly knees made the decision for her. She slid into the booth next to Zachary. "Let me call someone first." She made a quick call to Charlotte and told her she'd found Zachary safe and sound. Then she turned her attention back to Harlan. "Okay. Pick away."

Harlan's lips curved, eliciting another appearance of the dimples that she was beginning to find downright fascinating. "How about we get you two some lunch first?" He waved at Faith, the diner owner, who was wiping down the counter at the front. She smiled and waved back, tucking the rag under the counter and grabbing a menu from the holder on the counter.

"Your usual?" she asked Stacy, then bent to look Zachary in the eye. "And chicken fingers and apple slices for Zachary?"

Zachary nodded. "And can we get an apple for the horses?"

"I'll sneak one just for you." Faith smiled brightly at the little boy. She had a brand-new baby of her own, no doubt napping somewhere in the back. Stacy wondered how she did it.

The answer to her question emerged seconds later from the back of the diner, holding tiny little Kayleigh in his muscular arms. Faith's fiancé, Matt, cooed at the little girl, his face one big smile.

Matt spotted Faith standing at their table and made a beeline for her, looking nearly as besotted at the sight of her as he had been when he'd been talking to Faith's baby. "She laughed!" he announced without preamble. "I made her laugh."

Faith's eyes lit up. "Are you sure it wasn't gas?"

"It was a laugh! Watch." Matt made a silly face at the baby and, sure enough, little Kayleigh responded with a gurgling noise that sounded for all the world like a little chuckle.

Stacy felt a squirming sensation in her chest. Zachary had laughed at three months old. His first two years, he'd seemed normal in every way. His problems weren't obvious until later.

Faith grinned at Stacy and Harlan. "Did you hear that?"

"I did," Stacy admitted, smiling back at her and sending up a little prayer that Kayleigh would live a gloriously uncomplicated and happy life.

She glanced at Harlan, a little curious to see how he was reacting to the Kayleigh show going on beside their table.

He was looking down at his plate, his expression uncomfortable.

She felt another squirming sensation in her belly, this one hotter and queasier. So, Harlan McClain didn't like babies.

Or, she thought as she watched Matt bend and kiss Faith as if the rest of the world had disappeared for them, was it just the idea of happily ever after in general that Harlan found so hard to handle?

"Matt, hate to interrupt this nauseating display," Harlan said with a smile that Stacy didn't entirely buy, "but aren't you supposed to be working with Wade on those background checks I need by Friday?"

Matt shot him a black look. "Who died and made you Bart Bellows?"

Harlan's smile faded. "Someone's trying to kill the governor. I'd think that would be a top priority for everyone around here, not just Stacy and me."

Matt dragged his blazing black eyes away from Harlan's face to settle on Stacy's. He gave her a look of bleak sympathy. "I'll get back to it as soon as I finish lunch. Or are you the only one allowed to eat, boss?"

Harlan's expression softened. She thought she might even see a hint of red rising in his neck, as if he was aware he'd overstepped with Matt Soarez. "I'm sorry. Just having one of those days."

"Worse than yesterday?" Matt softened, too, turning the baby around to pat her on the back as she started fussing. "I don't imagine it was fun seeing the ex again—"

Harlan's gaze angled to meet Stacy's briefly, then turned

back to Matt. He forced another smile. "It was fine. She's getting married again, so I'm off the alimony hook."

"Really?" Matt grinned, seeming to take Harlan's answer at face value. Stacy was beginning to wonder whether all men had a touch of Asperger's syndrome, as bad as they were at reading subtext in conversations. "When's the happy day?"

"I don't know. Sometime soon. She said her lawyer would be in touch."

Zachary tugged at her sleeve, drawing her attention. "Mommy, we can't be late for the riding lesson today."

With a start of surprise, Stacy glanced at her watch. It was nearly one. The lesson started at one-thirty, and Zachary hated to be late for anything, but especially for his riding lessons. To her relief, she saw Faith approaching with their orders. "Faith, can we get that to go? I have to drive Zachary out to the Long K for his riding lessons, and you know how he is about being late—"

"Sure thing," Faith said with a smile of understanding, heading back toward the kitchen to prepare the orders for takeout. She dropped a kiss on her baby's downy head on the way, and managed a quick peck for Matt, as well.

"I'm sorry, Harlan—I have to take Zachary to the Long K. But he stays there for the afternoon and plays with the twins after his lessons, so I'll be able to give you my total attention until five. Okay?" Even as she asked the question, her stomach turned a little flip. After her scare earlier, the thought of leaving Zachary behind for someone else to take care of gave her the shivers.

"I have a better idea," Harlan said. "I'll go with y'all to the Long K. One of the ranch staff worked there before he worked at Twin Harts, so I was planning to talk to Lindsay about him anyway. We can work while Zachary is riding. Then we can all head back here when he's done."

She gave him a grateful look, certain that he'd been planning to talk to Lindsay by phone rather than drive out to the Long K Ranch. He must have read the hesitation in her expression earlier at the thought of leaving Zachary behind at the ranch. Maybe all men weren't bad at nonverbal cues after all. "Okay," she agreed.

She saw Matt Soarez give Harlan a thoughtful look. Matt's dark-eyed gaze drifted her way, and one eyebrow notched upward.

Stacy looked quickly away, not wanting to encourage Matt's speculation. Freedom was a tiny place, and it didn't take long for the grapevine to start rumbling around town. She should have realized that sitting down for lunch with Harlan McClain might start minds turning and tongues wagging.

And newly-in-loves were the worst. They thought everyone should be as happy as they were, come hell or high water.

Only being in love wasn't Stacy's idea of happy. Not anymore. She'd loved Anthony once, beyond all reason or sanity, and look how well that had turned out. Apparently Harlan's own marriage hadn't exactly been all hearts and flowers, either.

There weren't two people in Freedom, Texas, who belonged in a romantic relationship less than she and Harlan.

THE LONG K RANCH was smaller and a little shabbier than Twin Harts, which had benefited from the oil boom decades earlier. A month ago, during Wade Coltrane's investigation into threats against the governor, stories of a longtime rivalry between the Kemps of Long K and the governor's family had come out. Something about oil being found on land Lila Lockhart's father had bought from the Kemp family years back when the Kemps had suffered some financial setbacks.

If he had his choice, Harlan would rather be working at the Long K than at Twin Harts, he decided as he left the homey ranch house behind and walked down to the training ring, where Lindsay was giving Zachary his riding lesson. The governor's ranch was beautiful, but the Long K felt more comfortable. Like a real home.

He slowed his approach, his gaze following the dark-haired little boy as he circled the ring on a small but powerful-looking chestnut quarter horse. A ripple of unease tweaked his gut as he watched the tiny boy work the horse with a surprising show of both nerve and skill.

His gaze shifted until he spotted Stacy's dark hair dancing in the breeze. She stood at the corral fence, arms folded across the top rail. At first glance, she seemed at ease, but as Harlan stepped closer, he saw the worry lines creasing her forehead and the tense set of her shoulders and back.

He felt a powerful urge to erase those worry lines and relax her muscles. Maybe put a smile back on her pretty but troubled face.

He just didn't know if he had what it took anymore.

"He's good," Harlan said aloud.

She gave a little start, turning to squint at him. He stepped forward until he blocked the sun, and her face relaxed a little. "You have a habit of sneaking up on me."

He smiled and settled in next to her at the fence. "Sorry. Military training. Sneaking is second nature."

"What service?"

"U.S. Marine Corps, at your service."

"Oo-rah," she murmured softly. At his questioning look, she added, "My uncle was a Marine."

"Marine uncle, search and rescue father—what was your mother, a lion tamer?"

"English professor." She smiled, and he was struck again how much the expression transformed her face. The worry lines seemed to melt away, and her ordinarily pretty face became absolutely stunning.

He had to look away in order to continue. "I would ask who you're more like—your mother or your father—but I saw you in action in Austin."

"Actually, I have a master's degree in English," she said with a smile in her voice. "And a bachelor's degree in English and Poli-Sci. I was a few credits short of a PhD in English—thought I wanted to teach."

"What changed your mind?"

"I got married. My ex wanted me to pursue my interest in political science—he thought I'd be happier." She sighed, her expression bittersweet. "He was right, as much as I hate to admit it. I did some PR for a Tennessee congressman while I was working on my doctorate. Then Anthony decided Texas was the place to be if we wanted to make a big splash in politics."

"We?" he asked, looking back at the training ring as Zachary took the quarter horse into a canter.

"He's a lobbyist for the oil industry. Not really that political, actually—he follows the money. I was the one who was bitten by the policy bug."

He looked at her again, sensing from her tone of voice that her dangerous smile had disappeared. He was right. She was following her son's circuit of the ring with a troubled gaze.

"Enough personal stuff," she said. "Did you get what you needed at the ranch house, or should I call Lindsay over to talk to you?"

"I called ahead. Lindsay set me up with the foreman, and he gave me everything he had."

"Anything of note?"

"Maybe."

"What are you looking for in the background checks?"

"This and that," he answered vaguely, not sure he should be telling anyone, not even Stacy, about what Vince Russo had discovered about the explosive device. Information security might turn out to be vital to the investigation.

"I know it's important, but having people nose around in your background is creepy," Stacy murmured.

"You've been through it before."

"That's how I know it's creepy."

It wasn't his favorite part of the job, either. He usually preferred a more hands-on approach to security. Put a rifle in his hand, point him toward a nest of human vipers on the battlefield, and he knew what to do. Being in charge of all aspects of this security plan was a lot more daunting.

He flexed his scarred hand, the twinge of pain a reminder that his rifle-wielding days were behind him. He'd recently started taking target practice again, with mixed results. He supposed he should be happy he still had a hand left to pull a trigger. It could have gone the other way.

"How did you injure your hand?" Stacy asked.

"IED in Iraq," he answered shortly.

Her voice dropped an octave. "You're lucky to be alive. It's amazing you still have use of your hand."

"I know." At least, he knew that now. For months of painful surgeries, recovery and rehab at Walter Reed, he hadn't been so sure. Especially when his doctors told him he'd never be able to shoot his sniper rifle again.

He'd proved them wrong. Sort of. He could finally shoot again. He just couldn't always hit the target anymore.

"Is that why you retired from the service?"

"Something like that."

She looked up at him, her face once again transformed by a smile. Her skin seemed to glow where the sun touched it, as if she were made of pale gold. He felt tempted to touch the curve of her cheek to find out if she were soft and warm—or hard and cold. He clenched his arm to his side and looked away.

"What are we going to do about security checkpoints at the party?" Stacy asked. "I don't think the governor is going to want her guests to feel as if they've just entered the Green Zone in Baghdad."

"They're going to have to put up with at least some inconvenience," Harlan said firmly, glad to have business talk to distract him from how much he still wanted to touch her.

They continued discussing the plans for the fundraiser on the drive back to Twin Harts Ranch, their spirited back-and-forth punctuated now and then by Zachary's horse-related non sequiturs. They didn't make a lot of sense in the context of what he and Stacy were talking about, but Harlan found himself more amused than frustrated by Zachary's rambling commentary.

The kid was incredibly bright and articulate for a five-year-old, with a vocabulary and a logical thought process that might elude a much older child. And knowing his problem made it easier for Harlan to accept and enjoy Zachary for who he was. He was quirky and interesting. He was always going to be a different kind of person, but different wasn't always bad.

Sometimes, he thought, his gaze wandering back to Stacy's profile, different was very, very good.

THEY ARRIVED BACK AT THE RANCH around 5:00 p.m. "I need to get that ranch map you were asking about in the car," Stacy said as she let them inside the house. She headed for her bedroom office, leaving Zachary with Harlan in the living room.

It only occurred to her as she was coming back up the

hallway that she hadn't thought twice about leaving Zachary in Harlan's care. That wasn't like her at all.

She found him in the kitchen, opening a can of vegetable soup for Zachary, who sat at the kitchen bar watching him, perched on one of the tall stools.

Harlan glanced at Stacy over his shoulder. "He said it was vegetable soup night and he was hungry."

She smiled. "He insists on vegetable soup after his Thursday riding lesson. Not sure why."

"Hey, why question something good like veggie soup, right?" He smiled at Zachary. Zachary was stone-faced in response. To his credit, Harlan seemed unfazed by Zachary's lack of reaction.

"Is there a special way he likes his soup prepared?" he asked Stacy just as the phone started ringing.

She started toward the phone. "Use one of the bigger bowls to mix it with a half a can of water. Heat it for thirty seconds in the microwave, just to take the chill off. Put half in the red bowl—be sure it's the red bowl. I'll eat the rest later." Stacy picked up the phone receiver. "Hello?"

The line was open, but no one responded.

"Hello?" she repeated.

She thought she heard breathing on the other end, for just a second. Then there was a soft click and the line went dead.

Weird, she thought as she hung up the phone.

"Wrong number?" Harlan asked.

She turned and found him pouring soup into the red bowl sitting in front of Zachary. "I guess—nobody said anything."

A little furrow formed between Harlan's dark eyebrows. "Did you hear anything at all on the other end of the line?"

"I thought I heard breathing. It was probably some kid making a crank call." She shrugged it off.

"Maybe," Harlan murmured. He picked up the phone and punched a couple of buttons—checking incoming caller ID, Stacy realized.

"Anything?" she asked.

He shook his head, putting down the phone and heading back to the kitchen. "Number's blocked."

"Do you think it was something besides a prank?" Stacy settled down next to Zachary at the breakfast bar.

Harlan set the larger bowl in front of her and slid a spoon across the counter. "I don't think we can assume anything, one way or the other. Whoever's after the governor probably knows you're her closest aide. That could make you a target. I want to put an extra guard on your place, if that's okay with you."

Stacy had spent six years married to a man who had liked to micromanage her every move. To be caged that way again was unappealing. But the last thing Stacy wanted was for her son to be in danger.

"Okay," she said, looking down at her soup, all appetite gone. "But can you even get a guard here tonight on such short notice?"

Harlan was quiet for a moment. Stacy could almost see his thoughts churning behind his dark, conflicted gaze. Then his expression cleared and his jaw squared.

"Tonight," he said in a firm voice, "you'll have me."

Chapter Nine

Harlan listened to the sounds of Stacy putting Zachary to bed, feeling strangely lonely to be left out here in the living room, excluded from their nightly routine.

He'd been careful to keep his distance from them both that evening, not just to ease the wariness that lurked behind Stacy's dark eyes but also because he didn't want to throw Zachary's schedule into flux. He knew the little boy disliked change, and he didn't want to cause him any stress.

But he hadn't reckoned with Zachary's fascination with him. The boy had been Harlan's shadow all night, and only the promise of another ride at the Twin Harts stables later that weekend had coaxed Zachary away from Harlan's side at bedtime.

He should have called one of the other CSI agents to play bodyguard. Matt or Parker or Wade—someone already madly in love and immune to Stacy Giordano's considerable charms.

Which, he had to admit, he was not. He wanted her. He could admit that much, couldn't he?

Stacy emerged from the back of the house with a smile on her face and a stuffed horse in her arms. She handed the toy to Harlan. "Zachary sent you Bobbin in case you needed something to sleep with."

It's not Bobbin I want to sleep with, Harlan thought.

He forced himself to look away from her radiant smile. "Thanks. I just might."

She dropped into the armchair across from where he sat on the sofa, tucking her legs up under her. "I'm sorry he made a pest of himself tonight."

"He didn't. I like the little guy. He's really smart."

"Asperger's isn't all bad," she said. "He could have been born with severe autism and be unable to communicate at all."

"It must be expensive, dealing with his needs."

Her smile faded. "It's why I have to keep this job."

"Can't your ex pay more child support?"

"I could ask, and I will if I have to. But I depended on Anthony to be there for me and for Zachary, no matter what, and he failed me. That's one mistake I don't intend to repeat."

Harlan could sympathize. He'd counted on that same sort of loyalty from Alexis. Of course, now that he was a couple of years past her betrayal, he could see his own failures that had led to their divorce. But the big one—the infidelity—that was all Alexis. He'd never broken his vows to her until she shattered them by cheating.

"Do you really think that call was a threat?" Stacy asked.

Grateful for the change of subject, Harlan answered as truthfully as he could. "I don't know. I can't assume anything at this point."

"I wish we knew why the governor's a target. It would give us a better idea where to start looking for suspects."

"It could be anything," Harlan pointed out. "She's a woman—maybe someone doesn't think a woman should be president. It could be eco-terrorists or someone who doesn't like her Big Oil connections. It could even be far-right militia members who see her as another cog in the government machine."

"Could it be personal? Someone she's ticked off over the years?" Stacy asked.

"Maybe," Harlan conceded. "Do you know anyone who fits that bill?"

"Well, Henry Kemp, of course—he's always held on to that family grudge about the land purchase—but you've ruled him out now, haven't you?"

Harlan hoped so, since his fellow agent Wade Coltrane was crazy in love with Kemp's daughter Lindsay. "Anybody else come to mind?" He'd read over all the files by now and knew the governor was outspoken enough to draw fire from any number of special interest groups, but Stacy was in the governor's inner circle. She might know things the files didn't reveal.

"Allen Davidson can't stand her." Stacy grimaced. "He's a radio talk show host out of Dallas. They've crossed swords more than once. But I can't see him setting a bomb."

"Not even for higher ratings?" Harlan teased, making Stacy smile. His body tightened at the sight.

"There's also Bill Arkwright."

"The mayor?"

"He's not Lila's biggest fan. But does he dislike her enough to plant a bomb in Austin? Not seeing it."

"What about protestors? Have you come across any new groups lately?"

"The usual, really. Peace groups who don't approve of her support for military action overseas. Animal activists who don't like that she's a rancher and a carnivore. Environmentalists who hate her oil interests and her land management policies. Anarchists who hate government in general." Stacy shrugged. "You've probably seen all the files the state police have compiled on the various groups."

He had. None of them had stood out as blatant threats, although he supposed all of the groups might contain dangerous elements that weren't immediately obvious. "I guess, given the way Frank Dorian went after her, we should check on other death row inmates who were executed on her watch."

"We looked at the prison records after Frank Dorian went after Lila," she said. "There were 178 executions during her administration. The Texas Ranger Division is still looking into all of those and should have a threat assessment in a couple of weeks. Didn't anyone tell you about that?"

"You just did," Harlan said with a grimace. That many executions made for a lot of potential suspects. He had an old Marine Corp buddy who was working with the Texas Rangers these days. He'd have to give Steve a call and see if his old pal could pull any strings for him.

"You can't be an effective governor without making enemies." She shifted position until she sat cross-legged in the armchair. After dinner, she'd changed into a comfortable pair of knit pants and a faded Rice University T-shirt. It should have made her look a lot less sexy.

It didn't.

He nodded at the shirt. "I thought you were from Arkansas."

She looked down at the tee. "I went to Rice for college. Alabama for my master's. Vandy for my PhD—that's where I was working when Anthony decided we should move to Texas."

She really, really didn't care for her ex. He could tell from her tone of voice when she spoke of him. Of course, given what little he knew about the guy, he couldn't blame her. He wondered why she'd ever married him in the first place, but he didn't think he had a right to ask that question of her. After all, who was he to cast stones when it came to bad judgment in spouses?

But her mind seemed to move in the same direction, and,

apparently, she didn't mind asking questions of her own. "I couldn't help overhearing what you and Matt were talking about at the diner. Your ex-wife is getting remarried?"

He nodded. "She's marrying her divorce lawyer."

Stacy winced. "Ouch."

"We married young. And foolish."

Her smile was wry. "I wish I had that excuse. I was nearly twenty-six when I married Anthony. It was a whirlwind thing—my first serious relationship, really. I spent high school and most of college so immersed in my studies I barely looked up to notice the opposite sex."

He couldn't imagine how a woman as lovely and interesting as Stacy had managed to get through so many years of school without having a serious relationship or two. "Were you shy or something?"

Her eyes narrowed slightly, as if her mind were traveling back to her past. "Not shy. I was just really disciplined."

"Your parents were strict?"

"They were," she admitted. "They had reason to be. Not because of me, though. It was really about my older sister Tracy. She gave them a lot of trouble. Gave herself a lot of trouble, really."

"And they tried to make sure the same thing didn't happen to you?" he guessed.

"They didn't have to try hard. I saw the kind of messes Tracy got herself into. I didn't want that for myself. I guess maybe I went a little overboard with the self-discipline. I was terrified I'd do something to derail my goals."

"So how did Anthony sneak under your radar?" he asked with a smile, more interested in her answer than he liked to admit.

"I was twenty-six, burned-out and lonely," she answered, her cheeks flaming as if the answer embarrassed her. "He was smart, charming, sophisticated and experienced. I was completely unequipped to handle a man so determined and skilled at seduction." She met his gaze. "I asked him once, near the end of our marriage, why he'd chosen me out of all the women he could have pursued."

Because you're interesting and challenging, Harlan answered her question silently.

"He said he liked the idea of being with someone who'd never loved anyone but him," she answered with a bitter laugh. The sound made Harlan's stomach ache.

"He was an idiot, then," Harlan blurted, unable to school his tongue. He rose from the sofa, pushed by an urge he couldn't seem to squelch.

She rose, as well, like a gazelle startled into alertness by his swift movement. They stared at each other over the low coffee table, their gazes locked and blazing.

She was the first to look away. "I should get ready for bed. We have a lot to do over the next couple of weeks, and I need to get as much rest as I can manage with the schedule we'll be keeping."

"Yeah," he agreed, although he wanted nothing more than to follow her into the bedroom and do what his body was screaming for him to do. "I should probably take a walk around the perimeter, make sure everything's still."

They both moved at the same time, around the coffee table, and nearly collided. He put out his hand to steady her, his fingers brushing against her rib cage.

Her soft gasp sent need rocketing through him.

"Harlan," she murmured, her voice raspy and low.

Kissing her was the worst possible thing he could do at that moment. He knew it was.

He just didn't give a damn.

Dipping his head, he brushed his lips against hers. He kept the touch light. A question, not a statement.

She made a sound low in her throat and rose on her tiptoes, her mouth pressing back against his for a long, electric moment. Her hand flattened against his chest, her fingers curling in the fabric of his shirt.

Then she was suddenly halfway across the room, moving at such a fast clip she was in the kitchen before Harlan could do more than catch his breath.

She disappeared into the back of the house, her movements quick and nervous, reminding him again of prey trying desperately to escape the notice of a deadly predator on the prowl.

Hell, maybe that's exactly what she was.

Her escape leaving him feeling frustrated and edgy, he headed outside, glad for the chilly October night, which went a long way toward cooling the heat burning at his core. He took a couple of slow circuits around the house, keeping an eye out for movements in the dark. To the north, only a few lights burned inside the main house, but the white facade glowed in the moonlight like a pale wraith.

He made his way back to the front door of the guesthouse, feeling more in control now, although he still burned with anger at what Stacy had told him about her husband. What kind of narcissistic creep had he been to say such a thing to her? To make her think the only asset she could offer a man was her inexperience and her single-minded devotion to his needs?

Jerk.

He climbed the wide, shallow steps to the front door and halted just before he reached the landing, his gaze falling on something lying next to the woven welcome mat.

It was a deep golden bloom with four long petals. It looked freshly picked. He must not have looked down as he left the house, he realized. He'd been too busy trying to cool down his uncooperative sex drive.

He had no idea if it was possible to get fingerprints off

a flower. Probably not. And for all he knew, the bloom had blown here on the West Texas breeze that sometimes swept across the plains like a runaway train.

But if he was wrong...

He opened the front door and called Stacy's name. She appeared in the doorway, looking apprehensive.

He showed her the bloom. "Do you know what that is?"

Her expression shifted to curiosity. "A canna lily, I think." She bent to pick it up.

He bent, catching her hand to still her movement. She looked up at him, her eyes dark and intense.

He forgot about the flower. About the threat. About anything but how the Texas moonlight made her look more beautiful than anything he'd ever seen in his life.

He wanted to kiss her again, more than he wanted to take his next breath. And if the fire gleaming in her eyes meant anything, she wanted the same thing.

But she looked away, her struggle for control visible and ultimately successful. She stood, pulling her hand away from his grasp. "They grow in the governor's garden," she said in a strained voice. "Do you think it could have blown here?"

"I considered it." The porch light overhead wasn't on. "Can you turn on the light for me?"

A second later, the porch light cast its golden glow across the stoop. Harlan pulled out his cell phone and snapped a couple of shots, then took a pen from his jacket pocket and used it to flip the bloom toward him to get a better look. The flower had been pinched off, if the slight bruising on the pale green stem was anything to go by.

He rose from his crouch. "Could Zachary have pulled the flower from the governor's garden and brought it here?"

"No," she answered, her gaze still on the bloom. "He got

stung by a bee one time while smelling a flower. Now he has a phobia about flowers."

"Do you have a plastic zipper bag—like a sandwich bag?"

"Sure." She disappeared inside and returned with a clear plastic bag with a sliding snap closure.

Harlan used his pen to nudge the flower into the bag. He followed Stacy back into the house, watching to make sure she locked the door behind them. "I'll run this by the agency in the morning. Someone there will know if there's any way to get fingerprints off the flower."

She rubbed her arms as if she were cold, although the October night was unseasonably mild. "I don't know why I'm so creeped out by a flower."

"It's not just the flower," he said, almost reaching out to touch her before he realized what a bad idea that would be. He had to stay here tonight to keep watch. How much good would he be if he spent the whole time wishing he were naked with her in her bed?

That train's already left the station, McClain.

Too bad he hadn't gotten the number of the hotel in Amarillo where Alexis and her fiancé were staying. One two-minute conversation with his ex ought to be enough to cure him of his newfound fascination with Stacy Giordano.

Just thinking about his failed marriage helped him regain some of his equilibrium. By the time he settled on the sofa across from Stacy, he felt as if he might make it through the night without losing his mind.

"A flower is a strange means of making a threat, isn't it?" Stacy asked, after a couple of minutes of strained silence.

"Without a note, yeah. I guess it's an odd choice."

"Maybe it's not connected to what's happening with the governor at all."

"Have you received anything else like that? Like the strange phone call, or anonymous gifts?" he asked.

She shook her head. "I'm not really the type of woman who attracts secret admirers. I don't go out much, most of what I do is behind the scenes—"

"Maybe someone on the governor's staff?"

"I don't think so. I can't think of anyone who even gives me a second glance."

"Maybe you're so busy with your work, you're just not paying attention to who might be watching you," he suggested.

"You're creeping me out again."

"Sorry."

A weak smile crossed her face. "Well, not you. Just what you're suggesting."

"It could be a coincidence," Harlan said, although he couldn't put much conviction behind the suggestion. The flower alone might not mean much. Nor would the hang-up earlier. But coming so close together—and so soon after a deadly attack on the governor—Harlan couldn't help but see a connection.

He just didn't know how the pieces fit together.

Stacy went to bed a little after ten, after helping him turn the sofa into a narrow but surprisingly comfortable bed. After she had closed the door behind her, he pulled out his phone and called the CSI offices, planning to leave a message on the operator voice mail to let his fellow agents know where he was and what he was doing.

But Nolan Law answered the phone instead of the voice mail system.

"You're working late," Harlan said, although he wasn't really surprised. The first of Bart's Misfits, as Harlan had come to think of himself and his fellow CSI agents, Nolan was Bart's right-hand man. He was also the most enigmatic. From what little Harlan had been able to glean from the guy, he'd been badly hurt in combat, suffering burns that had resulted in extensive plastic surgery. He also claimed to have little memory of his life before his injury, although Harlan wondered if that was really true.

"Just catching up on some paperwork," Law answered. "What's up?"

Harlan told him about the possible threats to Stacy Giordano and her son. "I know it could be nothing, but she's a vulnerable point in the governor's defenses."

"Because of her son?"

"Hostage to fortune," he murmured. "She'd do anything to protect him. Someone who wants to harm the governor would almost certainly know that."

"Are you going to watch her tonight?"

"Yeah, but I can't be here all the time. I have to be on top of the whole security operation. I think we need to set up a checkpoint here at the guesthouse, as well. Do we have any more people on our most trusted list to add to the security detail here at the ranch?"

"I'll get on that and get you three more guys to take eight-hour shifts. I should be able to round them up by tomorrow morning if I start now."

"Thanks," Harlan said. He flipped his phone shut and stared up at the faint shaft of moonlight casting a pale streak across the ceiling.

He might have finally brought his body under control where Stacy was concerned—for the moment, at least—but his mind seemed to be charging full speed ahead, twisting in knots as he tried to figure out all the ways Stacy Giordano might be targeted by a clever assassin wanting to do harm to the governor.

There were at least two strikes against her—she was the governor's most trusted personal aide, and she was the mother of a vulnerable child with special needs. Someone ruthless enough to blow up a bomb in a crowd of innocent civilians was ruthless enough to use Zachary to force Stacy into a devastating act of betrayal. Harlan had no doubt that she'd do whatever was necessary, no matter the consequences, to save her son.

But would she be able to live with those consequences?

His stomach aching, Harlan made a silent vow. Whatever it took, he would find out who was trying to kill the governor. And he'd make sure nobody got close enough to Stacy to use her as a pawn. He just didn't want to look too closely at the real motives behind his determination.

Because the only thing more dangerous than the job he'd just taken on was the way he was starting to feel when he was with Stacy Giordano.

Chapter Ten

When Stacy walked into the empty living room the next morning around six, she found the place nearly spotless, cleaner than she'd left it the night before. The pillows and blanket she'd supplied to Harlan were gone. The dishes she'd left drying on the sink were now in the cabinets. Even the counter had been wiped down, erasing Zachary's sticky fingerprints. It was as if he'd never been there.

But she had a memory of a sweet, hot, too-brief kiss that assured her otherwise, even if she had no idea what she was going to do about it.

"Harlan?" she called aloud, though not too loudly for fear of waking Zachary. His preferred wake-up time was six-thirty. Any earlier—or later—and he'd be a bear to deal with, and Zachary trouble was the last thing she needed to deal with this morning.

Hearing the muted sound of voices outside, Stacy opened her front door and found Harlan, fully dressed, standing at the bottom of her porch steps, talking to a clean-cut Hispanic man wearing a leather jacket and jeans. They both turned at the sound of the door opening.

Harlan's expression was hard to read. He didn't look uninterested, exactly, but there was a sort of hardness to his gaze that caught her by surprise.

"Stacy, this is Rob Sanchez," Harlan said, nodding to the other man. "He'll be covering the seven to three shift."

Distance, she thought. That's what she was seeing in his eyes. He was putting a wall firmly between them after last night's brush with intimacy.

She should be glad about it, shouldn't she? Wasn't that what she wanted, as well?

"It's nice to meet you, Mr. Sanchez."

He extended his hand. "Rob's fine."

"Call me Stacy."

Harlan cleared his throat. "I've got to get out of here. I'm going to spend some of the morning at CSI, so I won't be back here until later in the day." He started walking away.

Damn it, she thought. He knew she couldn't leave Zachary alone in the house to chase after him. He was going to walk away without so much as a goodbye, after spending the night on her sofa, keeping her and her son safe.

After that tantalizing kiss.

Was she supposed to be okay with that?

Yes, Stacy. You are supposed to be okay with that, remember? You're glad things are going back to normal and that you don't have to spend another night dreaming about Harlan coming into your bedroom and reminding you what it's like to have a man in your bed again.

She swallowed a sigh and smiled at Rob Sanchez. "How'd he round you up so fast?"

"Corps Security called me last night around ten-thirty. They call, I come running." He cocked his head, giving her a look that wasn't entirely professional, though he didn't cross any lines that made her feel uncomfortable. "Do you need to know my credentials or anything?"

She shook her head. "If CSI hired you, I'm sure you're qualified." She slipped back into the house and closed the door behind her.

"Alone at last," she said aloud to the silent, empty room. And she felt every bit of the solitude.

"SANCHEZ MUST HAVE gotten there early." Nolan Law greeted Harlan when he walked into the CSI offices shortly after seven-thirty that morning.

"He did." Harlan shrugged off his jacket and hooked it on the back of one of the chairs at the conference table where Nolan sat. "Seems like a good guy. Where'd you find him?"

"He's one of Matt's Army buddies. Combat decorated, well-respected by his fellow soldiers and his commanding officers alike."

"Wonder why he didn't re-up?" If Harlan hadn't been pushed out by his own CO, he'd still be in the Marines himself. Maybe not as a sniper, but he could have found something else he could do. He had a bum hand; he wasn't disabled.

"Sanchez is the youngest in his family and the only boy. His mom's widowed now, getting a little older."

"Likes to have a man around to do guy kinds of things?" Harlan asked, his treacherous mind heading straight back to Twin Harts Ranch and Stacy Giordano's small, neat little guesthouse.

Stacy didn't want a man around. That much had been evident in their conversation about her husband.

But her kiss—that had suggested something else, hadn't it?

"Something like that," Law answered. He nodded his head toward the plastic bag Harlan was holding. "That the flower?"

Harlan laid it on the table in front of Law. Overnight in the bag, the bloom had lost some of its dewy freshness. "Any chance of getting a print off of that?"

"If it had been found at the scene of a mass murder,

maybe. But dropping a flower bud on a porch isn't a crime. Nobody's going to pay money for the technology it would take to get a print off that, not even Bart. Not unless you've got proof it's connected to the bombing."

Harlan sat across from Law, giving the small plastic bag a frustrated nudge. "I can't get it out of my head—Stacy Giordano is like a peach ready to pick. She's about as deep inside the governor's inner circle as you get. She lives alone, on the ranch, and has a son who's a handful to deal with."

"You think she could be bribed?" Law asked.

Harlan's gut told him no. "I don't think she's corruptible where money is concerned. But if someone were to threaten her kid, I don't think she'd let ethics get in her way. She'll do anything for her son."

"Well, we've got her under twenty-four-hour guard."

"But what about Zachary?" Harlan asked. "He could be snatched at school, or grabbed at his riding lessons, or hell, he could wander off at the ranch and get into God knows what kind of trouble." Harlan ran his hand over his head, wishing he had more information to work with. Something to tell him what direction the threat was coming from. Then, maybe, he'd be prepared when it happened.

"I hate to heap more bad news on you," Law said, giving Harlan a sympathetic look, "but apparently there's a group out of Austin planning to protest at the fundraiser. A group called Planet Justice filed for a permit."

"But the party is on the governor's personal property."

"That didn't stop the protestors down in Crawford a few years back, did it?" Law pointed out. "She's a public figure. People are going to protest. And from what little I know of Lila Lockhart, I'd say she'll probably want you to accommodate them. Free speech is a big damned deal with her."

Harlan suspected Law was right. The governor was exactly the kind of person who'd bend over backward to support constitutional rights, even at her own cost or inconvenience.

He supposed he'd have to bring up the subject with her as soon as he could set up a meeting. If he was going to have to contend with a crowd of protesters along with all the other threats he needed to anticipate, it was better to know it now rather than later.

He'd been crazy to let Bart and the governor talk him into this assignment—especially since it had been his curiosity about Stacy Giordano that had sealed the deal.

On top of everything else he had to contend with, Stacy was quickly becoming the most vexing complication of all.

ON FRIDAYS, Zachary stayed an hour late at Cradles to Crayons, working in a one-on-one session with Charlotte to improve his socializing skills, so Stacy didn't break for lunch until almost one. Before she headed into town, she walked down to the Twin Harts stables, dutifully signing in at every checkpoint, and stopped in, planning to thank the head groom, Cory Miller, for letting Zachary ride a couple of days earlier on such short notice.

Cory was out to lunch himself, but Trevor Lewis, the stable hand who'd taken Zachary out for the ride, was in one of the stalls, grooming a magnificent brown bay gelding. He smiled at her when she called his name.

"Hey there, Stacy. You in the mood for a ride?"

She smiled back. "No, just had a moment and wanted to thank you for letting Zachary ride on such short notice the other day. I really appreciate it."

Trevor gave the gelding's rump a gentle pat and came out of the stall, wiping his hands on his jeans. "He's a fun kid, once you get used to his ways. And he's real good with the horses. They all like him. Has a nice touch."

His words of praise for Zachary warmed her. It was

rare when people looked past his oddness to see the great kid underneath. She knew Zachary's problems would only get more challenging as he grew older, so the more people around him who understood who he really was, the better.

Of course, Trevor wasn't likely to be around in a few years, was he? Groom jobs at the stable were usually pretty short-term, until the holder moved on to a better paying situation. Trevor was in his late twenties, putting him a few years older than most of the other grooms who worked for Cory in the stables. Of course, with the economy as difficult as it was at the moment, the job might be more appealing now than it would be at other times.

"I feel as if I should pay you for the time you took with Zachary," she said aloud.

Trevor shook his head. "The governor pays us well enough already. Besides, taking Zachary out is like taking a break from work." He flashed her a smile full of unexpected charm, making her notice for the first time that underneath his overlong brown hair and layer of stable grime, Trevor Lewis was a nice-looking man. Though he was only a few inches taller than she was, his lean frame was hard-muscled and masculine.

In some ways, he reminded her a lot of her ex-husband, Anthony. Not in looks—Trevor's eyes were hazel, not blue, and his skin was a good deal fairer than her ex-husband's— but they shared a similar vibrant charm that had a way of catching a person by surprise with its intensity.

"You had lunch yet?" Trevor asked. "I'm about to head into town for something to eat. Would you like to join me?"

If she were a different woman in a different situation, it wouldn't be hard to imagine taking him up on the offer. He was, at most, no more than four or five years younger than she was, and his willingness to work a hard, dirty job was no mark against him in Stacy's book.

But now that she'd connected him in her mind to Anthony, there was no way she'd consider it. Deep down, she'd known that her marriage to Anthony would never last, long before he walked away from her and their son. She just hadn't wanted to admit that she'd been foolish enough to marry a man based solely on his dazzling charm and her own growing sense of time ticking inexorably away.

She stepped backward without even realizing she was going to do so, as if subconsciously she felt the need to put distance between herself and Trevor. "I already have plans," she answered, reassuring her conscience that lunch with her son qualified as a plan. "But you enjoy yourself."

"I will," he answered with the same smooth charm that had caught her attention a moment ago. If he was disappointed in her answer, he didn't show it. "Enjoy yourself, too."

She smiled in answer and walked away more quickly than she'd intended. By the time she was halfway back to the ranch house, she began to wonder if she'd been imagining the similarities she'd seen between Trevor and Anthony. On the surface, at least, they were certainly nothing alike. Anthony wouldn't be caught dead mucking out a stall or wearing grubby jeans and hair down to his shoulders.

Maybe she was just gun-shy where men were concerned in general. Her experience with Anthony had been one hell of a wake-up call for her in a lot of ways, not least of which was her bad judgment in men.

She'd thought him perfect, when he was anything but. She'd thought fatherhood would smooth the edges of his dog-eat-dog nature, but instead, his drive to be the best had apparently driven him to toss away the defective son—and the defective wife who bore him—so that he could find a better model.

As she neared the guesthouse, she was greeted by Lila's

campaign manager, Greg Merritt, chatting with Rob Sanchez at the new checkpoint. A splint encased Greg's left wrist.

"What happened to you?" She nodded toward the splint.

"Your boss took me riding yesterday. The black mare was feisty." His smile remained in place, but something Stacy saw in his eyes made her think Merritt wasn't entirely comfortable dealing with a woman like Lila Lockhart.

"I hope it's not broken." She fell into step with him as they walked to the guesthouse.

"Just a sprain." He glanced at her. "Guess you're wondering why I'm here."

"Well, yes. Do you need my help with something?"

"Actually, I need your car."

She arched an eyebrow at him. "My car?"

"The governor and Bart Bellows are meeting with a group of high-dollar donors this evening in Amarillo. We're trying to keep it very low-key—some of these donors aren't ready to tip their hands yet about their support for any of the party's candidates."

"And if you take my car, it won't draw attention from the press?" Stacy guessed. "Of course you can use my car."

"When was the last time you took it in for service?"

"I had the oil changed about a month ago, but the tires could probably use balancing, and I guess I should have the brakes and tires checked."

"Can you take it in today to have it checked out? The governor will need it around 4:00 p.m."

"Of course." She was planning on a quiet night with Zachary and his *Black Beauty* DVD anyway.

"Perfect. Just get the receipts for the service to the governor and she'll be sure you're reimbursed for the expense." Greg walked away without saying goodbye, pulling out his BlackBerry and punching in a number.

Rob Sanchez stopped him at the checkpoint, Stacy noted with amusement. Harlan McClain, or whoever at CSI had hired the young bodyguard, had good judgment in personnel.

She glanced at her watch—twelve-thirty. If she left now, she'd have time to leave her car at Hal's Garage for the checkup and service, walk to the day care to pick up Zachary and then take him to the diner for lunch. She pulled out her phone to let Hal's Garage know she was coming.

HARLAN HAD THOUGHT WORKING at the CSI offices that morning would make it easier to keep his mind on the work at hand and off of his growing attachment to Stacy Giordano and her son. But he'd spent most of the morning wondering what they were doing.

He knew Zachary would be at the day care, probably learning how to control his random chatter and the finer points of relating to his peers without freaking them out with his intensity and complete disregard for personal space. The kid was bright and interesting, and it would be a damned shame if his schoolmates treated him like a pariah. He had so much to offer, but kids could be cruel.

If Harlan was experiencing just this small amount of angst for the boy, what must his mother go through every day as she dropped him off at school?

No wonder she put up walls between herself and other people. Being Zachary's mother was a round-the-clock job she already had to share with her work for the governor.

Stop it. Just stop it. She's just an employee you're supervising. She's not bed-buddy material.

But when he entered Talk of the Town and spotted Stacy sitting at a booth near the counter, his whole body seemed to leap at the sight.

Zachary was with her, Harlan saw as he drew closer.

Zachary spotted him first, mostly because he was peeking his head around the booth to watch the other diners. His blue eyes widened when he saw Harlan, but he quickly went back to the task of scoping out the other customers.

Harlan figured for Zachary, that brief moment of recognition was as good as an excited greeting. He'd take it.

When Stacy caught sight of him, her expression was a bit more subdued. She gave a nod of recognition but didn't exactly make him feel welcome.

He supposed he deserved that for the way he'd left this morning without a goodbye. And if he were a smart man, he'd nod back and keep going.

But nobody had ever accused him of being smart.

"Everything going okay at the ranch?" he asked, stopping at their table.

"Fine," she answered flatly.

Zachary didn't say hello, but he scooted to the end of the booth and started playing with the sugar dispenser, making room on the bench for Harlan to sit down.

"Just you two for lunch?" Harlan asked.

Her lips flattened to a thin line, but she made the offer. "Would you like to join us?"

He felt a little guilty for forcing the invitation, but not guilty enough to refuse the offer. He sat next to Zachary. "Have you ordered yet?"

"Just our drinks. Molly should be back in a minute for our lunch orders." The cool tone of Stacy's voice made Harlan's stomach ache.

Figured. He finally found himself thinking of something more than sex with a woman and she was determined to cut him off at the knees. Of course, his hasty retreat that morning probably hadn't done much to endear him to her.

He cleared his throat. "I'm sorry I just hotfooted it out of there this morning. That was rude."

"You were there to keep us safe. You didn't owe us anything else. We appreciate it."

So formal, he thought. "That's not all it was, and you know it. Don't you?"

The pained look in her eyes showed her reluctance to have this conversation. But ignoring the attraction between them hadn't seemed to work very well so far. Maybe getting it out in the open and putting it to rest was the only solution.

"What do you want from me?" she asked.

He glanced at Zachary. "I want to discuss this in private, but since that's not an option, I guess I want to be honest about something. I'm not a good bet for happily ever after. Been there, done that, got burned."

Her lips curved slightly. "Same here."

"But that doesn't mean I'm not still a grown man."

"With grown man needs?"

He nodded.

"Is this some sort of proposition?"

"No," he said quickly, realizing he was botching this conversation royally. "I'm not proposing anything. I just thought we should get clear about what happened last night. I guess I'm asking what you want to happen."

"I don't want anything to happen."

He frowned at her quick refusal. Couldn't she have at least considered the possibilities before she nixed starting any kind of relationship? "Okay, then."

She gave him an oddly sympathetic look. "It's not that I don't find you attractive. I do. I'm just old enough and wise enough to understand the difference between wanting something and needing it. Whatever I might want where you're concerned, I know I don't need it. I don't need the complication or the headache. Can you understand that?"

Probably better than she knew. And he could accept it, he supposed. He just didn't have to like it. "I understand," he said. "And now that we're clear, maybe we can work in the same room without things getting so strange between us."

"Absolutely."

"A hug should only last for the count of three," Zachary commented from his end of the booth. He wrapped his arms around Harlan's waist and counted aloud. "One. Two. Three." He grinned up at Harlan and let go.

Stacy chuckled. "Charlotte's been teaching him some interrelational skills. How not to scare the other children."

"I could use a little training in that area, buddy," Harlan told Zachary. "What else did you learn today?"

Before Zachary could answer, the sound of sirens rose outside the diner. As the lunch crowd started moving toward the windows to see what was going on, Stacy's cell phone began to ring. She answered it, then listened for a couple of seconds to the speaker on the other end of the call. To Harlan's alarm, every bit of color leached from her face. "What?"

The doors of the diner burst open, and a pair of Freedom sheriff's deputies rushed inside. One of them, a tall, lanky man in his mid-thirties, barked out an order. "Everybody, we need to evacuate the area. If you're on foot, we've got a couple of vans outside. Otherwise, we want you to head east and gather at the Baptist Church on Mesquite. We'll let you know what's going on once we've cleared the square."

Harlan looked back at Stacy. Her eyes were wide and dark in her bloodless face. "What the hell is going on?" he asked.

She spoke in a faint, strangled voice. "That was Hal from the garage on the phone. They found a bomb attached to the undercarriage of my car."

Chapter Eleven

Even after two hours of talking to the sheriff's deputies, Stacy couldn't stop shivering, delayed reaction setting in with ruthless strength. "My son was in that car. Anything could have gone wrong—we could have hit a bump—"

Harlan wrapped his jacket around her, although she knew her chills weren't a result of being cold.

He'd been here with her at the sheriff's department ever since Jeff Appleton, the deputy who'd cleared the diner, had pulled her aside for questioning when they reconvened at the church. Harlan had insisted on coming along as a material witness, since he'd spent many of those hours with her.

Charlotte, bless her sweet soul, had volunteered to keep Zachary occupied elsewhere at the station while the sheriff's department investigators asked Stacy a thousand questions about the past twenty-four hours of her life.

"Maybe I should tell the deputies to call a doctor," Harlan suggested. "You may be in shock."

She struggled with the shakes, trying to get herself back under control. "No, I'm okay. I'll settle down in a minute. I just—I can't believe I was driving around with a b-bomb under my c-car."

His warm hands cradled her face, forcing her to look up at him. "You weren't in danger. Not yet anyway. It was rigged with a timer. It wasn't going to explode from an impact."

"A timer?" She ignored the urge to lean into his touch, though the temptation was almost more than she could bear. "How do you know?"

"I talked to Parker while the deputies were talking to you," he said in a quiet voice, shooting a quick look at the pair of deputies sitting just outside the waiting area where she and Harlan sat. "He has connections here and pulled a few strings for the information. This bomb looks a lot like the one you helped disarm in Austin, only this one wasn't rigged to blow with a cell phone call."

"When was it timed to detonate?"

"5:00 p.m."

She frowned, trying to make sense of what he'd just said. "Most days at five, it would be parked in the garage at the guesthouse. Would the blast have been big enough to take out the guesthouse, too?"

"I don't know. It would take out the car, and the garage would be destroyed, but the garage is brick, isn't it?"

"But my car wouldn't have been in the garage tonight," Stacy said, realizing that she hadn't even told Harlan about her reason for having taken her car to Hal's Garage in the first place. "Lila was supposed to take the car tonight. She and Bart were borrowing it to go to Amarillo for a meeting with potential donors." She told him about Greg Merritt's request. "They'd be on the road to Amarillo in the car at five. What if the bomb was meant for Lila?"

Harlan muttered a low profanity. "How many people knew about that trip?"

"I don't know. Not many—the whole reason they were taking my car was to keep the trip under wraps. The donors they were going to talk to aren't ready to commit to supporting the governor, and Lila didn't want the press to get wind of this and scare them off. I didn't even find out about it myself until this afternoon."

"Did you tell the deputies who interviewed you about the meeting?"

"Yes. I thought it might be important information."

He nodded. "I've got to make some phone calls. Are you going to be okay here for a minute?"

"I'm fine," she answered, trying to hold back the shivers that still rattled up her spine. She managed a weak smile. She could tell from his look of sympathy that he wasn't buying it, but he pretended to take her at her word and headed away from the waiting area.

A moment later, Jeff Appleton entered, holding a cup of steaming coffee. "How are you holding up?"

"I'm all right," she answered, suddenly overwhelmed by a powerful sense of paranoia, uncertain who she could trust anymore, after all she'd been through over the past few days.

She'd known and liked Jeff since she and Zachary had moved to Freedom when she took the job with the governor, but what did she really know about him? It had taken Charlotte to tell her that his daughter's developmental issues were the result of his late wife's drinking and driving. She'd never even thought to find out the details of his life herself, despite seeing him several times a week at the diner and around town.

She hadn't let herself get very close with anyone in town, had she? Everything in her life revolved around Zachary, and even the thought of anything approaching a normal social life was utterly exhausting.

Since her divorce, she'd never even looked at another man as a potential lover.

Not until Harlan McClain had swept into her life in the wake of a deadly explosion.

She took the coffee from him and took a sip. The bitter liquid burned a path down her throat, making her wince. But some of the shivers subsided almost immediately.

"I had Abby's sitter bring her down here. Just needed to see her, you know?" Jeff's smile was sympathetic. "Charlotte's watching her and Zachary in one of the interview rooms. Zachary's practicing his meet-and-greet skills."

Stacy chuckled apprehensively. "How's Abby taking that?"

"She thinks he's a hoot," Jeff said with a smile. "I don't think his quirks bother her much." He sighed. "I can see now that she's going to be a sucker for a pair of baby blues when she gets older. I swear, I'm shopping around for chastity belts as we speak."

"Hey, I have a kid with no concept of personal space," she said with a wry grin. "I can sympathize."

"Stacy?" Sheriff Bernard Hale himself stepped into the open doorway, his dark brown eyes sharp but friendly. He motioned with a jerk of his head for her to follow him.

She and Jeff walked with the sheriff down the hall to the same interview room where the deputies had questioned her earlier. But this time, it was full. Lila Lockhart sat at the table, flanked by Greg Merritt and Bart Bellows. Harlan and Parker McKenna stood behind them, their backs to the wall.

Sheriff Hale pulled out a chair for her and took the other empty chair beside her. "I've caught everyone up on what happened today. Now would someone like to catch me up on what y'all are doing about it?"

"Doing about it?" Bart Bellows answered the question with a fierce frown. "Hell, Bernard, I've practically handed the governor my whole stable of agents to keep her safe."

Lila patted his arm. "Bernard, I realize you've always been a little wary about having the governor living in your town, and I don't suppose I can blame you for that. I know having me here makes for a lot more headaches for you, and I don't imagine that'll get any better now that I'm running for president. But what would you have me do? Leave? I grew up here in Freedom. My parents before me, and my granddaddy's granddaddy helped build the first settlement, right down the road near Abernathy Ridge. Freedom's in my marrow."

"Of course I'm not suggesting you leave town, Governor." Bernard shot her a look of frustrated affection. "And I'm more than happy to have you fellows here, too," he added, nodding at Harlan and Parker. "All I'm asking is, keep me in the loop. The way you talked about the bombing in Austin when I asked you about it, you acted like it wasn't anything we needed to worry about up here. But I'm beginning to wonder if you were being entirely honest with me."

"Sheriff Hale, we can't be sure this was even about the governor," Greg Merritt said in a placating tone. "The bomb was attached to Ms. Giordano's car, not the governor's—"

Stacy shot him a black look. He knew damned well that the bomb, had it not been detected, would have killed the governor and Bart Bellows, not Stacy. He was trying to throw her under the bus to protect Lila's secret meeting that afternoon. She sneaked a look at the clock on the wall. It was only two. If they hurried, they could still be on the road in time to get to Amarillo. Was that all he cared about—massaging donors?

"We know about the trip to Amarillo," Bernard said flatly. "Ms. Giordano understood that we can't help keep the governor safe if we don't have vital information. I'm a little surprised you don't understand that, too, Greg."

Stacy saw Harlan's lips curve slightly at the sheriff's slightly scolding tone. She'd sensed from the beginning that Harlan didn't care much for Greg Merritt. She wasn't the man's biggest fan, either—he was far too ruthless and arrogant for her tastes—but he was a damned good political operative, and just the sort of campaign manager Lila needed to win, so she overlooked his personal flaws.

But had she overlooked too much? Lila had stolen him practically out from under Lloyd Albertson, her strongest competition for the party's presidential nomination. Could they be sure he wasn't a double agent, undermining her for Albertson's sake?

Harlan shot her a curious look, and she realized her turn of thought must be written all over her face. She quickly schooled her expression before the governor and Merritt read her mind, as well.

Within a half hour, Sheriff Hale had apparently exhausted his questions and he let them leave the sheriff's department. "We're going to have to impound your car for a few more days as evidence," Hale apologized to Stacy.

"I'll give her a ride," Harlan said quickly, shooting a look at Stacy. Something in his expression squelched her initial urge to argue.

"Could we get the booster seat from my car?" Stacy asked.

"I'll send one of the deputies to get it for you," Hale assured her. "You drive the Ford F-10, right, McClain?"

Harlan nodded, and the sheriff headed down the hall away from them, the governor and Greg Merritt right on his heels.

"I've lent the governor my car," Parker explained to Harlan and Stacy. "I'll catch a ride to the day care with Charlotte Manning and go home with Bailey."

Stacy squelched a smile at the eagerness in his eyes. Clearly, having to carpool with his fiancée was no hardship for the CSI agent.

She followed him and Harlan down the hall to the room where Charlotte and Jeff Appleton were entertaining the two children. Abby, Jeff's pretty, green-eyed six-year-old daughter, grinned at them as they entered. Zachary, as usual, kept working on his drawing, a look of steely determination in his blue eyes.

Stacy sighed. Trying to drag Zachary away from a project was always a pain. But to her surprise, he put away the drawing with only the briefest of protests, slipping his hand into Harlan's the second Harlan reached out to him.

He gave them a little more trouble, however, when Harlan tried to strap him into the booster seat attached to the narrow bench seat at the back of the truck's extended cab. "Where is your car?" he asked in a plaintive voice that reminded Stacy his nap was way overdue.

"My car is in the shop," she answered. "Remember?" He didn't have to know about the bomb or the impoundment, after all. "Mr. McClain is being very nice to give us a ride home."

Zachary wasn't impressed. "I don't like this truck."

"Well, you're going to have to get used to trucks if you ever intend to have a horse," Harlan said.

Zachary quieted down at the mention of the word *horse.* "Why?"

"Because a horse trailer is big and heavy, and not just any old car can haul it around," Harlan answered sensibly.

Zachary's forehead wrinkled with thought. Finally, his expression cleared and he got into the booster seat without further argument.

Stacy shot Harlan a grateful look, surprised by how well he'd handled Zachary's mini tantrum. Of course, compared to some of the doozies she'd dealt with over the past couple of years, this struggle had been nothing. She doubted Harlan would handle a full-scale Zachary meltdown quite as well.

Zachary fell asleep on the short ride back to the ranch. Harlan waited in the living room for her while she put Zachary in his bed and soothed him back to sleep.

Harlan smiled at her when she returned. "How are you holding up after all that mess?"

"I've had better days," she admitted. She still felt a little shaky, though the tremors had finally disappeared.

He reached out and straightened her collar, reminding her that she was still wearing his jacket. She started to shrug it off to return it to him, but he stepped closer and caught her hands in his. He twined their fingers together, his touch heating the air between them until she no longer felt chilled.

"You can't stay here alone." His half whisper should have sounded like a warning but somehow came out as pure seduction.

"I'm not really alone. There are guards all over this ranch." She hadn't intended to answer in a low, sultry tone, but somehow, there it was. She cleared her throat, but it didn't change a thing. "I'm okay."

"Maybe the bomb was intended for the governor, but we can't know that for sure." He let go of one of her hands and lifted his fingers to her face, brushing a tendril of hair away from her eyes. "You were also at the announcement in Austin. It was your car that was rigged for explosion."

"But the governor would have been in the car when it blew, not me." It seemed to take a great deal of effort to focus her attention on what she was saying. Whatever his fingers were doing to the side of her neck was as distracting as hell. The shivers she thought had finally left her returned in full force, driven by heat rather than cold this time.

"You said yourself you didn't even know the governor was going to borrow your car until earlier this afternoon." His finger traced lightly over the curve of her collarbone, sending a lightning bolt of fire straight to her core. She struggled to keep from closing her eyes and falling into his arms.

She had to get herself under control. She couldn't even remember what they were talking about.

She tried to step away from him, but her wobbly legs rebelled, sending her into a backward free fall.

Harlan caught her up in his arms, his body hot and hard against hers. His dark gaze scorched her, striking sparks along her nervous system. A muscle in his jaw worked furiously. "This is probably not the best time to suggest this," he growled in that same sexy half whisper, "but I think I should move in to protect you and Zachary."

For a second, the suggestion seemed the most sensible thing she'd ever heard. Of course he should move in here. He belonged here.

But that second passed, and the next brought doubts and fears crashing down around her.

She pulled away from his grasp. "No. That's a terrible idea. You know it's a terrible idea." She made herself look at him. "You know why."

"I'm the best person to do it. Zachary likes me. I like him. I'm working here anyway."

"You've already put guards outside my house. Twenty-four hours a day." She felt as if the room were closing in around her, squeezing out all the air until she couldn't draw a breath.

"And still someone set a bomb under your car," he pointed out sensibly.

She walked even farther away from him, seeking relief from the drowning sensation. She couldn't deal with this idea. She couldn't. If he moved in here, she'd lose control and do something stupid, just the way she had when she let Anthony blow into her life and sweep her off her feet, against all good sense. And maybe that would be okay if she was the only one involved. Sometimes, mistakes could be worth the price paid.

But she had Zachary to think about. Zachary who already liked Harlan more than he liked just about anyone else in his life, including her.

She couldn't let him pay for her mistakes any more than he already had.

"There's got to be another option," she said aloud.

"Will Zachary tolerate anyone else moving in?" Harlan asked.

"You don't even know if he'll tolerate you."

"He already asked me to move in."

She spun around to look at him. "What?"

"When you were talking to the deputies earlier, he asked me if I wanted to come stay with you. He thinks maybe he'd get to go riding every day that way. I could take him if you couldn't." Harlan's smile seemed genuine. "He's a bit of a plotter, your boy."

She leaned her elbows on the breakfast bar and buried her face in her hands. "You're using my son against me."

"I wouldn't do that," Harlan said sharply, making her look up at him again. He pinned her with a fierce gaze. "I would never do that. Not to Zachary or to you."

"But you're telling me this so I'll let you stay."

"I'm telling you this so that you'll understand why I don't think giving you a different bodyguard will work," he corrected.

"I'm not seeing much distinction," she muttered, even though she knew what he meant.

"It's just for a little while."

She shook her head. "You can't know that. We don't know who's doing it or why. You said you don't even know if the bomber is targeting Lila or me. There's no way to know how many more murder attempts there will be. What are you going to do, quit your job and become my full-time bodyguard? How much will you charge?"

He didn't seem to have an answer. Somehow, his uneasy silence was more frustrating than his earlier confidence.

She rubbed the aching spot over her right eye. "How certain are you that I need someone guarding me from inside my house?" she asked aloud.

"Very," he answered simply.

It was such a bad idea. She could see any number of ways things could go wrong if she agreed with Harlan's suggestion. Most of them ended up involving mind-blowing sex and deep regrets. But what if she said no and something happened to Zachary? What if her son died because she was afraid she couldn't resist Harlan for a few days?

What kind of mother was she if she couldn't put her son's welfare over her fear of her own desires and weaknesses?

"Okay," she said, straightening and forcing her gaze to meet his. "You can move in. But we need to set up some ground rules."

He narrowed his eyes. "I think I can guess one of them."

She didn't pretend not to know what he was talking about. "We've already agreed that things between us would never work. I don't think we need to test that theory in any way."

He frowned but nodded. "Strictly business."

"And you can't make unilateral decisions about my safety or my son's. You may be in charge when we're at work, but in this house, I make the decisions. Understood?"

"What if I can't reach you for some reason?"

She pushed herself away from the breakfast bar and approached him where he stood in the middle of the living room. "Then I'll trust you to do what's best for my son and me. But if I'm here to consult, you consult me. Don't try to hide anything from me, and don't try to overrule me."

His jaw twitched as if it caused him pain to agree, but he

nodded again, moving forward to meet her halfway. "Fair enough. I'll do all you ask. But there's one thing I need from you."

"What's that?" she asked, trying to pretend her body wasn't straining toward him, aching to close the few inches of distance between them.

He closed the distance for her, sweeping one arm around her waist. "You have to let me get this out of my system."

He bent his head and claimed her mouth in a hard, hot kiss.

Chapter Twelve

This is so, so wrong, he thought, even as he gave in to the fire licking at his belly and pulled her closer, molding her soft curves against his hard body until he lost track of where he ended and she began.

But damn, it felt right. Like she was made just for him, fitted perfectly to his shape. Soft where he was hard, filling in all the empty places inside him.

Her mouth drove against his with a hunger that caught him by surprise. She clutched his shoulders, her grip strong and fierce. He felt himself losing control of the moment, hurtling into a strange void where the ground beneath his feet disappeared, leaving him with nothing to hold on to but her.

No, no, no, he thought, panic beginning to set in. He couldn't let this happen. Not again.

He struggled for control until he felt the ground beneath his feet again. He eased himself away from Stacy, sucking in deep breaths until the wildfire inside him began to ebb.

She stared at him from the distance of a few feet, her eyes wide and as dark as bruises. Her lips were pink and swollen from his kiss, and it took every ounce of strength he could muster to keep from closing the distance between them again.

She cleared her throat. "Okay. Glad that's over with."

A bubble of laughter rose in his throat. Her lips curved in response, and a few seconds later, they were both laughing.

"That can't happen again," she said after the mirth subsided. "It just can't."

"I know." He meant the words, even as he was forced to silently admit that he didn't know if either one of them could control whatever it was that came to life between them when they were in the same room.

And now that he'd moved in, with no way out before the governor's fundraiser, keeping their distance was going to be harder than ever before.

"CARRIE RIVERS WANTS Vince Russo to coordinate with her own security," Stacy told Harlan Tuesday morning as they met in his office for a briefing. She felt a little flicker of pride in how steady her voice was, even though she was having trouble thinking about anything besides how good he smelled.

She'd sneaked a peek at his toiletries the morning after he moved in and saw that he really did use nothing but soap to shower and shave. She didn't find any shower gel or shaving lotion in his kit. Her father had been that kind of man, no frills, no fuss. He said what he meant and meant what he said, and when he'd died of a heart attack during a dangerous cave rescue, she'd felt a little piece of herself die with him.

She sometimes thought she'd been so vulnerable to Anthony's charms because he'd swept into her life only a few months after her father's death.

Was she falling into the same trap again with Harlan?

Not that he was anything like Anthony. Anthony had been wife-shopping when he'd spotted her at a political fundraiser years earlier. He'd never admitted it, but Stacy suspected he'd had a list of attributes he was looking for in a woman, and Stacy had fit the bill. Good academic record, clean background, calm temperament, pretty but not too pretty. Quirky backstory that could be exploited in the press—daughter of a college professor and a cave-diving daredevil who was equally at home in the halls of academia or the heart of an Ozark cavern.

Poor Anthony, she thought with a bitter half smile. He hadn't realized she was a lot like her father's beloved Ozarks—riddled with hidden depths full of secrets and surprises.

"I'm sure Vince will be happy to do that." Harlan shot her a wry smile. "Let me know when they plan to be in town and we'll set up a meeting."

"Actually, they're supposed to be in town this afternoon—Carrie has a show in Lubbock tomorrow night, and they asked if they could come by while they're in the area. Can Vince meet with them around three this afternoon?"

Harlan frowned but nodded. "Yeah, I think I can work them in. I'll call Vince and set it up."

"I also have a handful of names to add to the list of people who'll be at the fundraiser, too," she added, handing over the list she'd compiled during a meeting with the governor and Greg Merritt early that morning.

"I take it their trip to Amarillo went well in spite of the hullabaloo?" Harlan's fingers brushed hers as he took the list, setting off prickly sparks.

Living with Harlan had proved even more frustrating than she'd expected. Just being in the room with him could raise her temperature and send her thoughts careening into dangerous territory. And when their arms brushed while they were sharing kitchen duties, or when his fingers touched hers while passing her a spoon or a magazine, she found herself having more and more difficulty resisting the urge to have one more last kiss.

She dropped her hands to her lap, clasping her fingers together to stop their trembling. "The governor said it went better than she expected."

"That sounds promising." Something about Harlan's tone of voice made her wonder if he was talking about the governor's trip. But when he spoke again, his tone was back to normal. "What's on your agenda for the afternoon? Working from the guesthouse?"

"Zachary's riding with Trevor Lewis—one of the governor's stable grooms. It's his afternoon off, but he volunteered to take Zachary riding today so I can finish taking care of the hotel arrangements for Carrie and her people." She had felt a little wary about accepting Trevor's offer, afraid he might consider it a quid pro quo that would require her to do him a favor, too. But he had shown no signs of expecting anything from her, even turning down her offer to pay him for his time.

"Working on my off day makes me look good in the boss's eyes," Trevor had said with an engaging grin. "You and the little guy are doing me a favor."

She wasn't sure she believed him, not completely, but she was in no position to turn down the offer of a free riding session to keep Zachary happy and occupied while she took care of the work piling up on her desk.

"You sure Zachary's okay with this Trevor guy?" Harlan asked.

She looked up in surprise at the worried tone in his voice. "Yeah, he's fine. Trevor's taken him riding a few times before. He's good with Zachary, and Zachary's always happy to go riding."

"You know, you could always bring him here with you if you need to. I bought a couple of horse books to keep here." He waved at the bookshelf behind him, where two large picture books with horses on the covers lay on the top shelf. "I tried to find something I knew he didn't have at home."

His consideration touched her so deeply it nearly brought tears to her eyes. She blinked back the moisture, determined not to let her emotion show. As sweet as she found the gesture, she knew she couldn't take him up on it.

"That's really so considerate, Harlan. I appreciate your thinking of Zachary that way—"

"But?" Harlan asked, his brow furrowing as he caught the hesitation in her voice.

"But it's not a good idea for Zachary to get…too comfortable around you."

"Because of his Asperger's?"

"Well, yes. That's part of it," she admitted. "He forms crushes on people—he can be quite ruthless about it—"

"I think I can handle a five-year-old with a crush."

"I'm not worried about you. I'm worried about him."

Harlan looked a little insulted. "I would never hurt your kid, Stacy. I don't know what kind of person you think I am—"

"You wouldn't mean to hurt him. But if he gets too attached to you, too used to having you around, it'll be hard for him to adjust when you're gone again."

"I see." His frown didn't go away, but his gaze softened, and his voice held gentle sympathy when he asked, "How did he handle your husband going away?"

"Not well," she answered flatly. "It was sudden and we didn't have time to adjust." She realized too late that she'd said *we* instead of *he*.

If Harlan picked up on the slip, he was kind enough not to comment. "Little boys need daddies. Are you sure your ex doesn't want to see more of Zachary? Maybe he has regrets about the way he left."

"He has a new son," she said bluntly. "A perfect little boy

with his perfect new wife. He's just not really interested in revisiting the past now."

Harlan's mouth tightened to a line. "And he's in politics? Does he really think something like that isn't going to come back to bite him?"

"Oh, he pays his child support on time. He sends Zachary presents on his birthday and Christmas." The bitterness welling up in Stacy's throat tasted like bile. "I really don't want to talk about this."

"My wife cheated on me," Harlan said.

She looked up, not sure she'd heard him correctly. But the humiliation in his eyes suggested she'd heard him loud and clear. "I don't know what to say," she admitted.

"Not much to say, really." He sighed. "I never had a lot of money, growing up. My parents did the best they could, worked hard, but they barely had high school educations and there wasn't much either of them could to do to bring in a lot of cash. I never went without, but I had to make do a lot."

She nodded, understanding. There had been years like that for her, as well, until her mother finally earned tenure at the college where she was a professor.

"I met Alexis in the seventh grade, when my family moved to Snellville, Georgia, after my dad got a job at a trucking company there. She was the prettiest girl in school. Also one of the wealthiest. I had such a crush on her. All the way through to high school. When she agreed to go with me to the Homecoming game, it felt like winning the lottery."

Her first romantic date with Anthony had felt the same way, she realized. Magical, but sort of unreal, as if she knew deep down that it was mostly an illusion.

"I think our relationship must have been more a symptom of her rebellious stage than anything lasting and real," he murmured, leaning back in his chair and steepling his hands over his flat abdomen. "Hindsight and all that."

"How long were you married?"

"Seven years. We dated through high school and into college. She broke up with me her sophomore year and dated other people, but after graduation, when I came home from college for the summer before going to boot camp to fulfill my G.I. Bill commitments, she had just broken up with her latest boyfriend—some guy her father had seemed determined she should marry. Of course, to show her father who was really in charge, Alexis asked me to a party at the country club."

Ouch, Stacy thought. "And you didn't see through it?"

"Oh, hell no. She was prettier than ever, and I was about to head to Parris Island, then off to God knows where—on a global conflicts scale, we were somewhere between the Balkans and Iraq at that point, and I knew I had a good chance of seeing combat sooner or later. So of course I said yes. It might have been the last time I saw her. At least, that was my romantic take on things." He shot her a wry smile. "I didn't know it was going to lead to seven years of matrimony."

"Anthony swept me off my feet. We got married about three months after we met, then we had a big church wedding a few months later because Anthony thought it was important to have the big write-up in the paper and the photos on his desk at work. He was always very aware of appearances."

"Alexis, too. She came from money, and she had expectations."

Stacy nodded. "It's hard to fulfill people's expectations, especially if they're set in stone."

"She wanted me to quit the Marines as soon as I could. But I started rising in the ranks. I'd gone in as a private, and

I took to it like a pig to mud. I was good at it—especially shooting. I'd learned how to fire a rifle when I was a little kid in the Georgia woods, and the Marines needed snipers." He flexed his right hand, his gaze dropping to the web of scars radiating from a larger scar in the middle of his palm.

"You didn't want out."

"I'd found a job where I could make a real difference."

"That must have strained your marriage."

"You think I should have left the Marine Corps."

She shook her head. "I think you both should have probably compromised. Maybe you could have looked for a job in the Marines that wouldn't put you overseas all the time. And she could have accepted that you were a Marine for life."

"But I wasn't, was I?" He clenched his hand again. "Within a year of our marriage falling apart, I was out." He released a bitter laugh. "She should have hung on a little longer, huh?"

She couldn't see how their marriage could have been saved, given that his wife apparently thought it was okay to sleep with other men when she didn't get her way, but she wasn't about to say that aloud. She wasn't exactly in a good position to judge other people's marriages, was she?

"I'd contracted with a construction company to build a farmhouse in Walnut Grove, south of Atlanta. I wanted her to have a big house with lots of land so we could raise kids there together." His sad smile made Stacy's chest ache. "I had a week's temporary duty in Hawaii training sniper candidates, and at the last minute, they gave me an extra two days of R & R. All I wanted to do was go home and see how the house was coming. It was nearly finished—Alexis was already staying there...."

The ache in her chest spread as she realized what must certainly come next. "You wanted to surprise her?"

He nodded. "For future reference, that's almost always a bad move."

"She wasn't alone."

"She wasn't alone. And she was naked."

Stacy winced.

"So, that whole sad, sordid story was to say, no matter how bad you think your marriage was, it could have been worse."

She managed a smile, although the humiliation shining in his dark eyes made her want to hunt down his ex-wife and show her how an Arkansas girl dealt with cheating, lying hussies. "Noted."

"And now I need some air. What time do Vince and I meet with Carrie Rivers's security team, again?"

"Three," she answered, rising from her seat as he stood. "Would you like me to call Vince Russo for you?"

Harlan shook his head. "I'll do it. Listen—be careful this afternoon while I'm gone. I can probably arrange for one of the CSI guys to cover you until I can get back."

"I'm picking up Zachary from the stables at three, then working from home. I'll be in view of your security folks the whole time." She slanted a wry smile at him. "I promise I won't wander off."

He didn't return the smile. "You need to take the threat seriously, Stacy."

"I am," she assured him, growing sober. "I still think Lila's the main target, but people may try to get to her through me and my son. I get that."

"Good. I don't want to see anything happen to either one of you." Harlan walked her to her office. "Let me know if you have any trouble with the hotel accommodations."

"What are you going to do, yell at them until they fall in line?" she teased.

"I might," he answered with a grin.

She smiled back. "I think I can handle it without any shouting."

His expression softened, and he reached out one big hand and cupped her jaw, the touch tender and a little tentative. "Be careful," he said, his voice gruff.

"I will," she promised. It took every ounce of self-control she had not to turn her face into this touch.

The sound of footsteps around the corner made them both give a little start. Harlan dropped his hand to his side and backed away, letting her enter the office alone.

She closed the door behind her, something she didn't normally do, because she was afraid if she didn't close herself off to Harlan in some way, she'd end up following him outside and suggesting they get some air together.

She was still thinking about Harlan when she walked down to the stable to pick up Zachary after his riding lesson. Would it be so bad, really, to give in to the feelings she was fighting? Would it hurt anything to see where her attraction to Harlan—and his to her—could take them?

Anthony had crushed her heart, but Harlan wasn't Anthony. The more she got to know him, the more obvious that fact became. Harlan seemed to be crazy about Zachary— he'd bought him a couple of horse books, for Pete's sake. He asked about him all the time and he seemed to genuinely find pleasure in Zachary's company.

But was that enough to build a relationship on? His being nice to her son?

Zachary had so many other problems he'd have to deal with in his life. Screwing him up just because she was feeling lonely and needy was a great way to win Worst Mother of the Year.

She'd do anything for Zachary, give up anything for him. That was just how it had to be.

Trevor wasn't around when she got there, but Cory was

letting Zachary help him mix the feed for the horses when she walked into the big barn. She had to wait for Zachary to finish his task before he even acknowledged her presence.

"Did you have a good ride?" she asked as she walked him back to the guesthouse.

"Mommy, what's a bitch?"

Her steps faltering, she turned to look at him. "What?"

"Get the bitch out of my way." Zachary said the words in a gruff, mimicking voice. Then, in his regular voice, he asked, "Why is the bitch in his way?"

She crouched next to Zachary, alarmed. "Who said that?"

"The big man."

"Cory?"

"No. The big man." Zachary lifted his hand high over his head. "Why is the bitch in his way?"

"Zachary, that's not a nice word to say. It's a word that's meant to insult women, and it's a very mean thing to say."

"Why?"

She rose and took his hand, tugging him with her. "It's just not nice. It compares a woman to a dog."

Zachary was quiet for a few seconds. Then he asked, "Why is it bad to be compared to dogs? I like dogs."

"Dogs are great," she agreed, "but they're not women. I guess dogs might not appreciate being compared to people, either. Don't you think?" She tried to keep her tone light, though a thousand scary questions ran through her mind, starting with the most obvious: How had Zachary gotten near a big stranger who wanted someone out of the way?

"Where did you meet the big man?" she asked him, feeling a little flutter of relief when she spotted Rob Sanchez manning the checkpoint twenty yards from the guesthouse. He smiled at her and greeted Zachary with a handshake.

"Everything okay, Stacy?" Rob asked, making her wonder just how disturbed she looked.

"Yes, thank you, Rob." She tugged Zachary's hand when it became apparent he was thinking about lingering to pester Rob.

When they were safely inside the house, she sent Zachary to wash up in the bathroom and dialed Harlan's cell phone number.

He answered on the second ring, his voice low. "Can I get back to you? We're just finishing up with Carrie Rivers's security crew—"

"No, I don't think it can wait." She quickly told him what Zachary had said. "Am I crazy to feel a little freaked out by this? Someone he doesn't know—maybe someone we don't know—was talking about getting someone out of the way."

"No, you're not crazy," he said firmly. "Sit tight—I'm on my way."

HARLAN UNLOCKED THE FRONT DOOR of the guesthouse, glad to see Stacy had taken precautions. He found her pacing in front of the sofa, her expression full of anxiety.

"Where's Zachary?" he asked.

"In his room playing," she said, moving forward to meet him in the middle of the living room. When he held out his arms, she stepped into his embrace, pressing her cheek against his chest. He wrapped his arms around her, loving the feel of her body pressed to his in a way that had nothing to do with sex and everything to do with an overwhelming sense of completion.

She felt right in his arms. She fit.

"It's going to be okay," he murmured, and prayed he was right.

She gazed up at him, clearly wanting to believe. "I should have stayed at the stables and asked a few questions, but all I could think of was getting Zachary back home."

"Absolutely the right thing to do." He gently eased away

from her, lifting his hands to cradle her face in his palms. "I need to go talk to Cory—you said Zachary went riding with Trevor Lewis, right?"

She nodded.

He didn't want to leave her, but he had a job to do. With Rob Sanchez outside and Stacy doing a great impression of a mother grizzly on the inside, Zachary should be safe enough until he got back. "Lock the door behind me. I'll be back soon."

"Be careful," she said.

He touched her cheek lightly, then headed back outside.

"Is something wrong?" Sanchez asked as Harlan passed him.

"I hope not," Harlan replied.

But he couldn't shake the sense that a whole lot of trouble was coming their way, and fast.

Chapter Thirteen

"Cory Miller said he didn't see anyone with Zachary and Trevor, but they rode west and he didn't have his eyes on them the whole time." Harlan cut the truck engine and gazed up at the small apartment complex on the eastern edge of town. It was far nicer than the building where he and Matt rented apartments, he noted with surprise. Either horse grooming paid more than he realized, or Trevor Lewis had another source of income.

"It could've been another ranch hand," Parker McKenna said over the phone. "Zachary probably doesn't know them all by sight."

"But why was he talking about getting the bitch out of the way?" There was a measure of viciousness in the phrase that Harlan found chilling in light of everything else that had happened to Lila Lockhart over the past few days.

"I didn't say it wasn't troubling."

"If Lewis is at home, he's not answering his door. And I don't see his Honda in the lot." Harlan cranked his truck. "I've spent the whole afternoon trying to track down the guy, and meanwhile, Stacy and Zachary are alone."

"You don't think someone's deliberately sent us on a wild-goose chase, do you?"

"No—if Zachary hadn't randomly asked his mother about what the strange man said, we'd never even know about it." Still, he didn't like being away from Stacy and Zachary this long. Even if Lewis turned out to be harmless, Stacy and Zachary were still prime targets for whoever was coming after the governor.

"Let's move Lewis to the head of the background check list," Harlan told Parker. "Top priority."

"Will do." Parker hung up.

He called Stacy next. She answered on the second ring. "I haven't been able to track down Trevor Lewis."

"You don't have to," she answered.

"Why not?"

"Because he's standing right here."

WHEN HARLAN WALKED into the house, Stacy could see he didn't find the misunderstanding quite as humorous as she did. But she had to convince him Trevor was harmless before he started throwing punches and asking questions later. "Zachary misunderstood. It's really kind of funny—"

"What's he doing here?" Harlan asked softly, looking at Trevor, who sat on the sofa, looking at Zachary's favorite horse book with her son.

"He went back to the stable for something and Cory mentioned you were looking for him. He came here to find you."

"And you let him in?"

"He was horrified Zachary misunderstood what had been said."

"Who was the big guy?"

"Trevor says it was one of the new cowboy hires—Trevor and Zachary ran across him during their ride. He was repairing an old fence in the lower pasture. What the guy actually said was 'get that pitch out of the way'—the pitch he and another cowboy were using to weatherproof the fence."

Harlan glanced at Trevor again. "Damned convenient."

"I do know that old fence was due to be fixed. Maybe you could check into that tomorrow?"

"I've put Trevor to the front of the background check list," Harlan murmured.

"You must be the guy who's looking for me."

Stacy turned to find Trevor standing only a couple of feet away, his hand outstretched.

Harlan hesitated, then shook Trevor's hand. "Stacy just told me what happened." He gave a nod toward the door. "If you don't mind, I'll walk you out. I have a couple more questions."

Stacy made a face at Harlan as he and Trevor went outside, hoping he'd read her warning expression correctly. The last thing he needed to do was rough up one of the governor's employees over something as stupid as a little boy misunderstanding an innocent comment.

"Trevor said I could go riding again tomorrow," Zachary said from the sofa.

"Zachary, you're already going riding this Friday, remember?"

"But he said I could go riding. He's good with it."

Still on edge, despite Trevor's reassurances, Stacy lost her cool. "Zachary, I'm not good with it. You can't do everything you want to do just because you want to do it. Sometimes you have to make compromises."

Zachary rolled onto his back on the sofa, kicking the cushions. "I have to ride tomorrow. The horses depend on me!"

"I think the horses can do without you for a day."

"No, I promised I'd go riding." He started flapping his arms against the sofa cushions. "I promised."

Stacy closed her eyes and counted to ten. "Zachary, we can talk about this later."

"I promised! I promised the horses, Mommy. I promised the horses. I promised the horses."

"Okay, Zachary, we'll talk about it tomorrow."

"You can't break a promise, Mommy. Remember? You can't break a promise. I promised the horses. I promised them, Mommy." He was crying now, his words coming out in hitching sobs. He was approaching meltdown, and fast.

Stacy went to the desk by the window and pulled out a binder she kept there. She took it over to Zachary, who was writhing on the sofa, still crying about his promise to the horses. "Remember our schedule?"

"I promised."

"Tomorrow, we're supposed to spend the day at home, see?"

He sniffled but paid attention when she showed him their visual calendar for the week. Wednesday was their at-home day, symbolized by a photo of a house. "You know how you don't like to change our schedule."

"But the horses need me! I promised."

The front door opened and Harlan entered. Stacy felt her stress level rise another notch as he stopped in the middle of the room, staring at Zachary's tantrum with a look of growing concern. *Welcome to the world of parenting aspies,* she thought, turning her attention back to her son.

"We're going riding Friday. I'll even take the afternoon off Friday so I can be there to watch you the whole time. But I can't take off tomorrow afternoon."

"Why not? I promised the horses!"

"I have to work."

"Can't you work another time? The horses are expecting me." Zachary hadn't worked himself back up into shouting again, but she could see the signs.

"Zachary, why don't we discuss this later? Wouldn't you rather go to your room and watch your horse show DVD?

You don't even have to take a nap this afternoon if you'll go watch the DVD. How about that?"

Sniffling, Zachary nodded. "I promised the horses," he reminded her as she walked him to his bedroom. But he went inside and pulled the DVD from his shelf. He knew how to work the machine by himself, and she knew what he needed right now was to be alone, doing something he enjoyed, to reduce the stress that was working him up to a meltdown.

Rubbing her temples to fight against the headache starting to throb behind her eyes, Stacy returned to the living room and almost bumped into Harlan.

He caught her elbows to steady her. "Is he okay?"

She nodded, dropping her hands, which forced him to let his own hands fall away. She found herself missing the touch. "Too much change in his routine over the past few days. It's a lot of stress for an aspie."

He frowned. "Aspie?"

"It's what people with Asperger's syndrome call themselves. A lot of adult aspies think it's the rest of us who are weird. They call us Neurotypicals."

He grinned. "I like that. Who says everybody has to think the same way?" He headed into the kitchen.

Her eyebrows lifted with surprise. "Says the guy who used to march and chant in step with the rest of his unit."

"There are benefits to working in unison," he admitted, pulling a glass from the cabinet. "Want some tea?"

She shook her head. "I don't suppose Zachary will ever be in the military. He likes structure, but let the drill instructor give him an unexpected order, and he'd fall apart."

"Is that why he was upset? You changed something on him?"

"He made plans to ride at the Twin Harts stable without asking me. Promised the horses, you see, and you're not supposed to break a promise." She settled on the bar stool, watching him pour a glass of tea. "How did the talk with Trevor go? Do you believe his version of things?"

"I don't know." Harlan brought the tea over to the counter. The only thing between them now was the breakfast bar.

Stacy was struck by a sense of intimacy she hadn't felt with anyone in a long time. By the end of her marriage, she and Anthony were more like acquaintances than friends, much less lovers. But with Harlan, she felt...connected, somehow. She was beginning to think of him as someone she could count on to be there for her when she needed him. It was a dangerous conceit.

"You still think he might be up to something?" she asked.

"I don't know. His story sounds plausible. I'm definitely going to want to look deeper into his background. I'm not sure I'd let Zachary go riding with him alone anymore, either."

"I'm afraid I'm not going to be able to talk Zachary out of wanting to ride tomorrow afternoon."

"What do you have to get done tomorrow?"

She rattled off a long list of responsibilities. "We're working against the clock anyway, and I can't expect everybody else to work harder just to accommodate Zachary's obsessions."

"How about this? Some of that stuff you can do from here, after hours, right?"

"Yes, but someone has to get Zachary fed and bathed and ready for bed—"

"I can do it."

She shook her head quickly. "It's too much to ask."

"You didn't ask. I offered."

"But why?"

"Because it will help you and Zachary." His eyes darkened, and the air around them crackled with heat. "Let me help you."

Blinking back the hot tears stinging her eyes, she nodded. "Okay. I'll only take off as long as it takes to drop him off and pick him up."

Harlan shook his head. "No, go riding with him. You do know how to ride, right?"

"Yes, but—"

"It'll make his day. And he'll be safer out there if you're with him." Harlan reached across the space between them and slid his fingertips along the curve of her jaw, making her shiver. "Zachary's not the only one around here who needs a break from all the stress."

She took a swift breath through her nose, fighting tears again. This time, she wasn't able to stop them from spilling.

Harlan came around the counter and pulled her into his arms, his large hand curving around the back of her head in an awkward yet tender caress. "It's okay," he murmured. He seemed out of his depth, somehow, as if her sudden emotional breakdown scared him to death, but the fact that he was making an effort to comfort her anyway made her heart contract with an overwhelming rush of affection.

He was a man in a million. If she were any other woman, in any other situation, she'd be crazy not to snap him up before another woman figured out what a prize he was.

But she wasn't another woman. And this wasn't another situation.

She eased away from his embrace, swiping at her tears with her fingertips. "I'm sorry about that. I'm okay now."

"Why don't you go wash up? I'll check the fridge and see what I can rustle up for dinner."

She couldn't hold back a watery smile. If Harlan wanted to play nursemaid to Zachary over the next couple of days, he needed to know a little of what it would entail. "Tuesdays are hot dog night. No mustard. And exactly twelve potato chips for Zachary. No more, no less. He likes apple juice with hot dogs. Not tea, not milk—apple juice. I have juice boxes in the fridge—that will do. And he only eats hot dogs from the small green plate."

Harlan gave her a look of pure panic, but he nodded. "Is there a list somewhere? For when I watch him alone."

"I'll leave you one," she promised.

He smiled his relief, making her heart skip a beat.

A man in a million, indeed.

"WE'RE WAITING FOR some information from California— Trevor Lewis grew up in San Mateo, but he's been working as a horse groom throughout the Southwest for several years." The second Harlan walked into the CSI offices on Wednesday, Vince Russo greeted him with a sheaf of notes he'd been working on all morning. "Lewis seems to have a good record with the stables where he's worked here in Texas. We have preliminary info from stables where he worked in Arizona and New Mexico. Hopefully more by this afternoon."

"And the stuff from Cali?"

"Probably tomorrow. Might be in the evening, though. Our California contacts aren't very quick to respond."

"Maybe we need new California contacts," Harlan grumbled. "Where's Coltrane?" Wade Coltrane was an experienced undercover agent, and Harlan had decided he needed someone on the inside of the governor's staff.

Vince looked at his watch. "Halfway through his vows."

"His vows?"

"He and Lindsay eloped. They decided a big wedding would take too long, and besides, when you already have four-year-old twins, why wait?" Vince grinned. "They found a little bed-and-breakfast up in Lubbock that had a wedding chapel nearby. Carrie thinks it's the most romantic thing she's ever heard of. I have a feeling it's going to be hard to surprise her when it's our time to get hitched." Vince had fallen hard for the country music star when he'd been tasked with protecting her a couple of months earlier. *Another CSI bachelor bites the dust.*

"Why am I always the last to know about anything that happens in this place?" Harlan asked. Some investigator he was.

"You've been a little busy."

"Yeah." Harlan took the notes Vince gave him to his desk and settled into the leather office chair, leaning back until the chair springs creaked. He looked over the notes, trying to find patterns that might give him a better idea whether Trevor Lewis was just an ordinary guy who worked at a stable or if he was a real threat to Stacy and Zachary.

And the governor, of course, he added with a mental kick to his own backside. He'd been hired to protect Lila Lockhart, first and foremost.

But he couldn't quite make himself accept that anyone's safety was more important than Stacy's and Zachary's.

"There was one thing in those notes that nagged at me, but I haven't figured out why," Vince said, rolling his chair closer to Harlan's desk. "When Trevor Lewis was working on a ranch outside Melrose, New Mexico, he asked for a week off in the middle of foaling season. He'd been working there less than six months and didn't have vacation time built up, so he took the time off without pay."

"I think he has an independent source of income," Harlan said, filling Vince in about Trevor Lewis's apartment. "It's nicer than yours or mine. Rent at that apartment complex is close to a grand or more a month—I priced it when I was looking for a place to live."

"But why take off during foaling season? What did he need the time off for?"

"I don't know," Harlan admitted. "What was the date?"

"March 21."

Didn't ring any bells. "Maybe I'll ask Trevor that question the next time I see him." He'd talked to Stacy a few minutes before he walked into the CSI offices and learned she was on her way to the Twin Harts stable. He'd checked Trevor Lewis's schedule—he got off at three on Wednesdays, so Stacy and Zachary should be safe enough. She said she was going to ask Cory Miller to take them out.

As long as she stayed away from Trevor Lewis, she should be just fine.

STACY HAD ASSUMED she could ask Cory to take her and Zachary out riding on Wednesday afternoon, but the stable manager wasn't there when she walked Zachary down that afternoon. Only Trevor and a couple of other grooms were around.

"The governor and her daughters wanted to check out the south pasture," Trevor explained. "They came here about a half hour ago and wanted Cory to show them the improvements he was making to that area, since they're thinking of adopting several shelter horses out of the Houston SPCA. They want to make sure we have enough places for them to roam safely."

"Well, that's okay. I can stay today, so I'll take Zachary riding myself."

Trevor returned the stall rake to the tool rack on the barn wall. "I'm about to clock out, so I'll come with."

Apprehension fluttered through Stacy's stomach. "That's not really necessary. I'm sure you have better things to do with your afternoon."

"Nope, not a thing." Trevor grinned at Zachary. "Ready to help me saddle up Alamo?"

"Alamo is an Appaloosa," Zachary told Stacy, tugging her hand for her to follow him to a nearby stall. He looked up at the horse standing at the stall door, beaming. "Alamo's spotting pattern is a blanket with spots pattern," he told her, lifting his arms for her to pick him up. She had to hold on tight as he lurched toward the horse, petting the animal's dark nose.

"You've been reading up on your Apps, haven't you?" Trevor ruffled Zachary's hair. "Let's get Alamo saddled up."

"He looks awfully big," Stacy said as Trevor brought the gelding out of the stall. He wasn't a particularly tall horse, but his shoulders were wide and powerful, and his rump was even larger, with thick, muscular hindquarters that marked him as a quarter horse. "Are you sure this is the horse Zachary should ride?"

"Ah, he can handle old Alamo. Can't you, Zachary?"

"Let's go!" Zachary wriggled from Stacy's grasp and hopped to the ground, running over to pat the Appaloosa's shoulder.

She knew that the horse's wild-eyed look was typical of Appaloosa horses, but she couldn't tamp down a bubble of panic rising in her throat. "Zachary, maybe we should wait until another day to ride—"

"Mommy, I promised!" Zachary's voice rose dangerously.

"Okay," she said quickly, wishing Harlan were here to talk to. She felt pushed, trapped by the constant threat of a Zachary meltdown and Trevor Lewis's breezy confidence that Zachary could handle anything Alamo could hand him.

Trevor chose a friendly palomino mare named Delta for Stacy, while he saddled up Soldado, a feisty chestnut gelding, for himself. "We'll take it at a walk until we reach the east pasture, then we can let them canter a bit."

"I'm not sure Zachary's ready for cantering."

Trevor met her nervous gaze with a smile. "Relax, Mom. Zachary's been cantering for a couple of weeks. Alamo is an easy ride, and Zachary's doing great with him."

She had to admit her son's physical coordination was better than a lot of aspie children. Charlotte attributed it to the physical therapy Stacy had started Zachary on once the Asperger's syndrome was diagnosed.

"I'd just prefer he keep it to a walk."

"Horses like to run," Zachary said with a tug of the reins, expertly guiding Alamo through the stable door and out into the yard. "I have to let him run. I promised."

She was going to have to have a long talk with Zachary about making promises.

HE WAS JUST MAKING UP an excuse to see Stacy, Harlan knew, but he told himself it was concern for her and Zachary that drove him back to the ranch around three. A car accident on the highway that bordered Twin Harts Ranch slowed him down, delaying his arrival, so he bypassed the main house and drove directly down the access road to the stable, stopping to ask the guard at the checkpoint if he'd seen Stacy and Zachary.

"They left about five minutes ago with one of the grooms."

"I thought they were going with Cory Miller."

The guard shook his head. "Miller took the governor and her daughter to see one of the lower pastures that's been reclaimed. Ms. Giordano went with one of the younger grooms."

The first hint of alarm fluttered in Harlan's gut. "Do you

know which one?" But even before the guard answered, Harlan knew what he'd say.

The guard checked the sign-in sheet. "It was Lewis. Trevor Lewis."

Chapter Fourteen

The sweet-natured palomino, Delta, was a comfortable ride, though Stacy was sure she'd be sore in the morning. It had been a while since she'd been riding, but the walk to the east pasture was a pleasant reminder of one part of her life she'd left behind when she became a time-consuming combination of Zachary's mother and Lila Lockhart's aide-de-camp.

She'd grown up riding horses in Arkansas—some of her father's rescues had required him to be able to travel by horseback, so he'd bought a couple of strong, reliable packhorses and kept them in a barn behind their house.

Though Jupiter and Mars had been friendly, dependable trail mounts, they loved to be run. Stacy was one of their favorite people, because they knew that, more often than not, when she saddled them up she was going to let them run like the wind across the pastureland behind the family home.

"See? He's a natural," Trevor called, nodding toward Zachary, who was handling Alamo with more confidence than Stacy had expected. He rode ahead and settled next to Zachary. "Ready to show your mom what you can do, cowboy?"

Zachary beamed at Stacy, his joyous look making her heart skip a beat. But before she could even smile back,

Trevor gave Alamo's rump a light slap and the horse kicked into a canter.

"Trevor, have you lost your mind?" She gave the palomino a quick tap of her riding boot to urge her forward. If the Appaloosa gelding decided to break into a gallop, Zachary could be hurt or even killed.

"Let the boy be a boy!" Trevor turned his horse into her path, forcing the palomino to pull up.

"Get out of my way!" Stacy pulled the palomino to the left to ride around Trevor.

Trevor blocked her again, laughing. "Stop being such a mother, Stacy! Let him have fun! He knows what he's doing—"

"Damn it, Trevor, get the hell out of my way!" She whipped Delta's reins to the right and sent her into a gallop, flying past Trevor. He grabbed for the reins but she kicked out at him, catching him in the thigh, and he wasn't able to stop her.

Zachary was over fifty yards ahead of her now, holding on to the back of the galloping Appaloosa like a baby monkey clinging to its mother. Stacy couldn't tell if he was in control or not, and she hadn't gone ten yards before Trevor caught up with her, reaching again for the reins.

"Will you stop fighting me?" he called out, flashing her a confident grin as he snagged the reins to slow her horse. "Zachary's tougher than you think. You don't have to baby him all the time. You put so much time in mothering him, you don't even seem to remember you're a beautiful, vibrant woman!"

She stared at him, stunned by his gall and appalled by the accompanying compliment. "Are you even listening to yourself?"

Trevor's grin widened. "You're so sexy when you're angry. Did you know that?"

Her skin crawling, she jerked at the reins, trying to regain control. "You don't know me well enough to say any of these things to me."

His grin faded, but he held on to the reins. Stacy looked away frantically, trying to keep an eye on Zachary, who was racing farther and farther from where she was struggling with Trevor.

"Let go of those reins or I will tell the governor about your insubordination."

His eyes narrowed to slit. "Insubordination? That's how you see me, isn't it? Just some lowlife shoveling horse crap for a living. Right?" He laughed, but the sound was anything but humorous. "You don't know anything about me, Stacy. And if you want to tattle, go ahead. I don't need this job."

He still held the reins. Stacy gave a tug. "Let go."

He tugged the reins tighter, pulling their horses together until his leg and Stacy's almost touched. "Does the governor know how often you bring Zachary riding?"

She gritted her teeth. "Let. Go." She kicked her horse, hoping Delta's strength would wrench the reins from Trevor's hands before she had to resort to something more violent.

The ploy worked momentarily, and she and the mare thundered across the pasture, heading north to try to cut off Zachary and the Appaloosa, which had started to curve back around as they neared the outer edge of the pasture, where the land began to rise subtly.

But in seconds, she heard hoofbeats drumming toward her, catching up fast. "Does she know, Stacy?" Trevor called after her. "Does she know how hard the job is for you?"

She felt his hand touch her elbow, grabbing for her. He tugged sharply, and she clamped her knees around the horse, trying to keep her seat as he pulled her off balance.

Suddenly, he let go. She heard the sound of a scuffle

behind her, and even her fear for Zachary couldn't keep her from looking back to see what had happened.

She saw Harlan on the ground, holding Trevor down on his face, his arms pulled behind him to subdue him. Nearby, a black horse danced and snorted, eager for more action.

"Go!" Harlan said urgently, and she turned and goaded the mare into a flat-out run.

Alamo was still running a half circle around the edge of the pastureland, galloping with all the joy and power of a young, healthy horse given his head. She feared Zachary would fall from the saddle at any moment, but when she reached the gelding and caught his reins, Zachary was laughing with wild joy.

"Did you see me, Mommy? Did you?" Zachary threw himself into her waiting arms, almost overbalancing her. He wrapped his arms and legs around her as tightly as he'd wrapped them around the horse. "Alamo ran like the wind, Mommy. Like the wind!"

She buried her face in his neck, fighting tears of relief.

"WHAT DO YOU MEAN, there's no reason to hold him?" Harlan stared at Jeff Appleton, stunned. "How about child endangerment, for starters?"

"Zachary is fine." Appleton looked regretful but resigned. "And since Stacy doesn't want to press charges—"

"What?" Harlan shook his head. "No way."

"It's my word against his." Stacy's voice sent a dart of awareness shooting through him, as if his whole body was becoming acutely attuned to her—her voice, her expression, the way she always smelled good, like a light breeze on a warm spring day. At the moment, she was all stony determination, the muscle in her jaw tight and twitching. "And this kind of mess is the last thing the governor needs now."

"I have to go process Lewis out of here." Jeff gave Harlan another apologetic look and headed down the sheriff's station hallway, leaving Harlan and Stacy alone in the corridor.

"Stacy, that guy could have gotten Zachary killed."

Her eyes flashing, she spoke through gritted teeth. "Don't you think I know that? Believe me, I'm not going to let Zachary go anywhere near Trevor Lewis again. But Jeff said Trevor's talking about pressing assault charges against you—"

"That's bull—the guy was trying to manhandle you."

"The governor and Greg think—"

"Greg." Harlan spat the name, glad that the governor and her smarmy campaign manager were nowhere nearby. "I know the guy's supposed to be some sort of political genius, but he shouldn't be facilitating that creep's attempted blackmail."

Stacy put her hand on Harlan's arm. Even blazing with anger, he wasn't immune to the feel of her fingers on his skin, his flesh quivering where she touched him. "The party is tomorrow night. That's our priority. After that, the governor and I can talk about finding other reasons to fire Trevor Lewis. Ironclad reasons he can't use to smear her in the press."

"He threatened that, too?"

Stacy's lips pressed to a thin line. "Let's just go home. I have a ton of work to do." Her expression softened, her lips curving. "And I believe you promised you'd watch Zachary for me."

He let his own anger drain away, making the effort to do as she asked—table any thoughts about Trevor Lewis until after the fundraiser. He'd already put Trevor at the top of the background checklist—if the CSI team found anything that showed Trevor was a real threat to the governor or Stacy and Zachary, they'd call him immediately.

Besides, she'd just suggested they go home, and he liked the warm, tingling feeling the word gave him when she said it.

"Okay. Where's the little cowpoke?"

Stacy smiled. "Sitting on Sheriff Hale's desk, telling him how to tell the difference between an Appaloosa and a dapple."

That's my boy, Harlan thought, grinning as he followed her down the hall to the sheriff's office.

"ZACHARY, WE HAVE TO be very quiet. Your mama's working."

Harlan's voice trailed down the hall from Zachary's room, making Stacy look up from her paperwork and smile. They'd eaten an early supper and Harlan, true to his word, had coaxed Zachary to play with him in Zachary's room, leaving Stacy free to finish up the last-minute calls and arrangements she had to make for the fundraiser.

"She's always working." Zachary's plaintive voice carried even farther than Harlan's, sending a little arrow of guilt straight through Stacy's heart.

"I know. She works very hard," Harlan agreed. "And do you know why?"

"No."

Harlan's laugh echoed Stacy's soft chuckle at her son's answer. "She does it so you can go riding and go to school and learn what Miss Charlotte teaches you. And so you can depend on there always being hot dogs on hot dog night—"

"Tonight was peanut butter and jelly night."

"I know. And your mother works hard so she can buy your peanut butter."

"I don't like crunchy peanut butter."

"Well, good," Harlan said with a chuckle. "That way, there'll be more for me."

Zachary laughed at Harlan's joke, catching Stacy by surprise. Zachary almost never knew when to laugh at other people's jokes. But somehow, Harlan had broken through to him for that one small moment. Stacy blinked back the sudden sting of tears.

"See, some people have to do stuff they *don't* like to do in order to be able to do the stuff they *do* like to do," Harlan explained.

"Why?"

Harlan laughed again. "I've been asking that question since I was a little kid like you."

Zachary sounded incredulous. "Wow. That's a long time!"

Stacy smiled, trying to picture Harlan's expression in response to her son's honest if unflattering comment.

"Yeah, I reckon it is," Harlan conceded. "And, best I can tell, the only answer to that question is, that's just how things work."

"I don't like that answer." Stacy could picture the look of disapproval on her son's face just by the tone of his voice.

"Yeah, me either," Harlan agreed. "So, come on, Zachary, my man—where did we leave Beauty?"

A few minutes of reading later, Zachary's murmuring narration slowed and finally stopped. Stacy smiled at the silence; Zachary had fallen asleep in the middle of reading, as he often did.

After a couple of minutes more, Harlan emerged from the bedroom, looking a little rumpled but smiling. "He reads better than half the guys in my platoon."

"He fell asleep?"

"And right in the middle of an exciting part, too." He wandered around the living room for a few seconds in fidgety silence before he finally edged over to where she sat and looked down at her.

"What?" she asked, laying down her pen.

"I wish you'd reconsider pressing charges against Trevor Lewis." Harlan crouched beside her desk, his dark eyes intense and serious.

"He has more cause to press charges against you than I have to press them against him." She turned her chair to face him. "I don't like the idea that he wins this round, either, but I've learned in this business, you have to pick your battles."

"I hate politics," he growled, pushing to his feet and walking a few feet away. "Politics get in the way of getting things done."

"Politics help you enact the policies that get things done," she countered, though the words sounded hollow even to her own ears. So much of what she'd believed her entire life had been challenged over the past few years.

"Maybe in the big picture sense. Maybe." He crossed back to her, his expression passionate. "I get why there are rules. Hell, I was a Marine. I also get why you have to try to do the best thing possible for the most people involved. I do. But when you're the guy who falls between the cracks as a result—" He clamped his mouth shut, turning away once more.

"We're not talking about what happened with Trevor anymore, are we?" She walked over to where he stood at her front window. Outside, night had fallen in earnest, only pale moon glow tempering the inky gloom.

He angled his gaze to meet hers. "Not entirely."

"You fell through the cracks?"

"Probably not an apt term." He flexed his right hand.

She caught his hand in hers, turning it over to look at the network of ragged scars marring the skin. "Does it still hurt?"

"Just aches sometimes." His voice deepened. "Probably

the scar tissue pulling or something. There's a bit of nerve damage, so I don't have full feeling in that hand."

The temptation to kiss the center of his scarred palm nearly overwhelmed her. "What did you do in the Marines?"

"Worked hard. Tried not to get killed. Pretty much what every other guy in a uniform did in Iraq." His lips curved in a self-protective grin. "Sort of like motherhood, huh?"

She returned the smile. "Yeah. But it's worth it."

"Zachary's such a great kid. I'm starting to get why aspies believe it's the rest of us who have the problems. We're the ones who lie about our feelings and try to temper everything. Zachary just says what he thinks and lets the chips fall where they may. World might be a better place if more people just told the damned truth."

He wasn't just saying that to make her feel better, she realized. He wasn't trying to play an angle or manipulate her the way Anthony might have done in the same situation.

The tears she'd been fighting ever since the run-in with Trevor burned their way into her eyes. She blinked, trying to keep them at bay a little longer. "I hope he always has people in his life who feel the same way about him. I think if he does, he'll be okay."

Harlan lifted his hands to her face, his thumbs brushing over the moisture seeping from her eyes. "As long as he has you, he'll be okay."

Unable to bear the gentle sympathy in his gaze, she pulled away from his grasp. "I should get back to work."

"What's left to do for tonight?"

Nothing, really. Harlan had helped her out more than he knew by taking care of Zachary while she was tackling the last-minute calls to finalize the arrangements for the party the next evening. "I'm sure I can find something that needs doing—"

He caught her hand as she tried to turn away, his grip warm but strong. "Anything to avoid being alone with me?"

A low groan of frustration escaped her throat. "Why do you have to make it so much harder? I told you how impossible it would be for us."

"Why?" He caught her other hand, tugging her closer.

The pull of him was like a powerful undercurrent, dragging her inexorably further out to sea no matter how hard she fought against it. "I have to think of Zachary."

"Zachary likes me."

"Too much," she protested. "He's too attached to you already, and the more time I let you spend with him, the harder it's going to be when you're not here any longer."

"What if I'm not going anywhere?"

Hope jolted through her at his words before she could squelch it. "You won't be here after the party, will you?" she argued. "You'll be going back home and Zachary and I will be alone again."

"I'm not Anthony," Harlan growled.

"I didn't say you were—"

"That's how you treat me," he shot back, dropping her hands and pacing away from her, his movements quick and full of pent-up frustration. "'I can't let Zachary get close to you because you'll hurt him.'" He whipped back to face her. "Just like Anthony, right?"

She took a couple of quick steps toward him before she could stop herself. "You're nothing like Anthony."

Closing the rest of the gap between them, he cradled her face between his hands again. "Then don't treat me as if I am."

She tried to remember what it had felt like when she realized her husband of seven years was leaving her because she'd given him what he'd considered a defective son. The pain had been crushing, though in retrospect, she could admit that most of the hurt was for what he was doing to their son.

But all she could remember was the sound of Harlan's voice, full of affection and appreciation for her beautiful, difficult son. All she could see was the fire smoldering in his eyes right now, as he gazed at her as if she were the most desirable creature in the world.

She closed her hands over his wrists, sliding her fingertips lightly over the muscles and tendons there until her touch elicited a soft gasp from his lips.

Rising to the tips of her toes, she brushed her lips against his, a shaky breath escaping her throat.

Fingers tangling in her hair, he brought her closer, deepening the kisses until she felt drunk and fevered. She felt something hard and flat against her back—the wall, she realized in a haze of heat and need. He'd pushed her up against the wall. And she liked it. The fierce passion of what they were doing, the reckless abandon, the promise of fire and pleasure.

Why had she fought so hard against this? As Harlan's hands dropped to her hips, tugging her flush against his hardness, she knew she couldn't keep fighting something she wanted so much.

She dragged her lips away from his long enough to say, "We can't wake Zachary up."

Harlan nuzzled his way to her ear to whisper, "Umm, how hard a sleeper is he, anyway?"

Arching her neck to give him better access, she slipped her hand between their bodies and released a soft laugh as he uttered a low groan in response to her touch. "You're a Marine. You know how to be stealthy, don't you?"

He caught her hand, threading his fingers through hers and tugging her toward the hall to the bedrooms. "So we're at war?" His blistering gaze met hers.

She closed the bedroom door behind her and turned to face him, unable to stop a smile of sheer exhilaration. "Not anymore. Now we're just negotiating the terms of surrender."

Harlan reached for the top button her blouse. "Who won?"

"Who cares?" She kissed the curve of his jaw.

Laughing, he picked her up and carried her to the bed.

Chapter Fifteen

A trilling sound woke Harlan from a dead sleep. Instantly awake, he oriented himself with the ease of a well-trained Marine. Nighttime. Indoors. Beautiful woman sleeping naked by his side. The ringing continued, louder by the second.

Easing himself from Stacy's bed, he grabbed the cell phone from his discarded jeans. "Yeah?"

"Why are you whispering?" Vince Russo asked.

Harlan tucked the phone under his chin and pulled on his jeans. Once outside the bedroom, he spoke in a more normal voice. "Sorry—I wasn't in a position to talk."

Russo was quiet for a second. Harlan could only imagine what he was thinking.

"Is something up?" Harlan prodded.

"Yeah, something big. I can be at the ranch in ten—"

Harlan glanced toward the hallway, a flood of sizzling memories swamping his brain for a second. When she'd finally fallen asleep in his arms, spent and trembling, she'd looked so happy. Somehow at peace for the first time since he'd met her. He wanted that feeling to last for her.

"No." Holding a CSI strategy meeting in the middle of her living room would definitely be a mood-killer. "We'll meet at the office—twenty minutes."

Grabbing a clean set of clothes from the hall closet where he kept his things, he headed to the bathroom.

"THE GUY HAS KEPT a low profile for the past ten years," Vince Russo told Harlan a half hour later in the CSI conference room. Parker McKenna was there, along with Nick Cavanaugh and Nolan Law. Cavanaugh was a silent, thoughtful man in his mid-thirties, though Harlan knew there was a lot more to him than his demeanor might suggestion. In Iraq, Cavanaugh's recon talents had been legendary, though his last scouting expedition had ended in a deadly ambush.

"But?" Harlan prodded.

"But we finally reached a family member who didn't close ranks," Nolan Law told Harlan. He passed along an enlarged photograph. "This is a photo from the Transworld Trade Partnership summit two years ago."

The photo showed a group of young men and women dressed in black. Most wore balaclavas or scarves over their faces, but the camera shot caught one man in the middle of donning his mask. Harlan recognized the stable groom immediately. "Lewis."

"He was part of a black bloc protest at the summit, and you know what kind of trouble those guys can cause," McKenna said.

Harlan nodded. Black bloc tactics were often part of antiglobalization protests, designed to create havoc and thwart the efforts of law enforcement to control crowds of protestors.

"According to his cousin, he's very much involved in anarchistic antiglobalization protest groups, including Planet Justice," Nick Cavanaugh answered.

Harlan raised an eyebrow. "The group protesting the fundraiser tomorrow?"

McKenna glanced at his wristwatch. "Tonight, you mean."

Harlan eyed the clock on the wall. Almost two in the morning. Man, he'd give almost anything to be back in bed, cuddled up to Stacy's naked curves. But he pushed the tempting thought away, focusing on the job at hand. Keeping the governor safe would keep Stacy and Zachary safe, as well. "I've tried to talk the governor into enlarging the buffer zone between the protesters and the ranch, but she won't have it."

"Either speech is free or it's not," McKenna murmured.

Harlan knew he was quoting the governor; he'd heard her say it enough times. "And if it's not, why the hell do we pretend to be Americans?" he finished the governor's favorite saying.

"I appreciate the sentiment," Law said, "but I don't think we can be stupid about it. I don't like the idea of a Planet Justice operative working on the governor's staff."

"How do we know he's still with the group?" Russo asked.

Harlan gave him a look. "What are the odds he's not?"

"Not good," Russo conceded. "But how do we get him out of there, given what happened today? The governor fires him, he'll say it's to keep him quiet about your assault on him."

"I barely touched him," Harlan said with a grimace. "I think we have to do this aboveboard. I think knowing he's recently been a member of a group protesting the governor's fundraiser should be enough to warrant an extra look."

"Planet Justice has been known to set explosive devices," Russo said. "There was a protest in Chicago during a free trade conference. The cops found a couple of pipe bombs set near the venue entrance. They tied the bombs to a couple of Planet Justice operatives, though the rest of the group publically denounced their actions."

"Would that be enough to get a search warrant for Lewis's apartment?" Harlan asked Law.

"Worth a try."

Jeff Appleton had given Harlan his cell phone number earlier at the sheriff's station. He knew the man had a six-year-old kid, but Harlan didn't think this call could wait. They had under twenty-four hours before the fundraiser.

He pulled out his cell phone and dialed Appleton's number, wondering where they'd find a judge willing to sign a search warrant in the middle of the night.

"Mommy?"

Stacy's eyes popped open at the sound of her son's voice. It took a second to reorient herself, because even though she was in her own bed, nothing felt normal. Her legs and arms felt sore, as if she'd worked out for hours, and she was completely naked beneath the tangled sheets.

She slanted a quick, panicked look to her left and saw with relief that Harlan was no longer there. Normally, after the best sex she'd had in, well, ever, she'd be a little miffed to wake up alone, but with her son staring at her from the side of the bed, she was happy to be alone.

She just hoped Harlan didn't walk back in here from the bathroom or kitchen or wherever he'd wandered before she was able to coax Zachary to go back to bed.

"I'm hungry," Zachary said.

"Zachary, you had a big PB&J sandwich for dinner."

"But that was hours ago," he complained. "I'm a growing boy and I need food."

She couldn't stop a smile. "What do you have in mind?"

"Why are there clothes on the floor?"

"I was tired," she answered quickly, checking to see if

Harlan's clothes were there, as well. She didn't see his jeans, but his shirt and underwear were on his side of the bed, thankfully hidden from Zachary's view. "Tell you what, go get your robe on—it's cold in here. I'll get mine on and we can go see what we can find in the fridge, okay?"

While Zachary went to retrieve his robe, Stacy slipped on a T-shirt and a pair of yoga pants, topping them with her own fuzzy terry cloth robe. Not exactly the most flattering of looks, but if Harlan was going to be part of her life, he might as well get used to seeing her how she really was, right?

Part of her life, she repeated silently. Harlan really was going to be part of her life, wasn't he? Why had she been so afraid of letting him in? He wasn't anything like Anthony or any other man she'd known, except maybe her father. And her dad had been as strong and reliable as a man came.

A giddy sense of joy percolated at the back of her mind as she waited for Zachary to return. She knew it might take a while—Zachary could dither over the choice of clothes longer than a teenage girl. Something else Harlan would have to get used to, although he already seemed to be doing a great job at accepting and even appreciating Zachary's idiosyncrasies.

Zachary finally appeared in her bedroom doorway. "I think I want a grilled cheese sandwich," he told her solemnly, as if he'd spent a great deal of time contemplating the perfect choice. Which, knowing Zachary, he probably had.

She headed down the hall with her son, fully expecting to find Harlan sleeping on the sofa. After their lovemaking, before she'd fallen asleep, he'd asked her if she thought he should go back to the sofa, since Zachary was so resistant to any little change in his routine. She couldn't remember her answer, but it was just like Harlan to think about what would be comfortable for her son.

Only Harlan wasn't on the sofa. Or in the kitchen. And the bathroom in the hallway had been dark when they passed it.

Her sense of joy began to fade into unease when she glanced out the front door and saw that his truck was no longer parked out front, the way he'd left it the night before.

Where on earth had he gone?

THE FIRST GRAY LIGHT of dawn was peeking over the flat horizon in the east when Harlan's cell phone rang. He was sitting in front of the picture window in Jeff Appleton's living room, wishing he were back at the Twin Harts guest ranch, skin to skin with Stacy, but he'd promised to stay at Appleton's place to keep an eye on his daughter while Jeff went on a mission to get the sheriff and a local judge involved in the latest break in the investigation into the Austin bombing.

It was Appleton. "We got the warrant. We're about to execute it now."

Harlan felt a rush of relief, followed almost immediately by an anxiety chaser. What if they found nothing incriminating at Trevor Lewis's house? Would he blame the invasion of his privacy on the governor? Call it a vendetta against him?

Harlan could very well be making things a lot harder for Stacy, he realized as he settled back down to wait for word from Jeff Appleton. And that was the last thing he wanted to do.

He wished he could call Stacy and tell her what was going on, at least to forewarn her. But it wasn't yet four in the morning. She wasn't likely to be awake at this hour, and if he called, he risked waking Zachary, as well. Stacy didn't need the added stress of dealing with a sleepy, cranky little boy.

Hopefully, the search would be finished by dawn, and Harlan could wake her with a kiss and the good news that Trevor Lewis was no longer a threat to Zachary or anyone else.

Then what? After tonight's fundraiser, his job with the governor was over. She hadn't mentioned adding him to her permanent staff, and after the stress of dealing with the politics of her position, Harlan didn't think he was interested in such a job.

Really, the only draw at all was being with Stacy and Zachary, and since he had no intention of leaving Freedom as long as the two of them remained there, he could see her and Zachary whenever she'd let him, couldn't he?

After signing the divorce papers and putting his disaster of a marriage to Alexis behind him, he'd sworn he would never make the foolish mistake of marrying again. And until he'd met Stacy, he hadn't met a woman who'd tempted him away from that vow for a second.

But Stacy was different. She was tough and loyal and as trustworthy as a woman came. And if he could just convince her that he wasn't going to flake out on her the way her jerk of a husband had done, maybe they really had a shot at happiness.

At least, he hoped so.

But first, they had to figure out who was gunning for the governor. Because as long as that threat remained, Stacy and Zachary would never really be safe.

RULE ONE, STACY THOUGHT, *is to be cool about it. No crying, no recriminations, nothing that'll make you look like a loser.*

Even if you are.

The hours since Zachary woke her had passed slowly,

unaided by anything approaching actual sleep. She'd tried to go back to sleep after Zachary was finished with his snack and safely tucked under the covers again, telling herself she was overreacting to finding Harlan gone when she awoke. But as the sleepless hours ticked away, the truth seeped through the barrier of self-protective lies she'd constructed.

It had been sex. Good sex—no, great sex—but that was all it had been. It hadn't been the start of some wonderful new relationship. It wasn't going to be the first of a lifetime's worth of nights spent curled up in Harlan McClain's strong arms.

And the sooner she dealt with those facts, the sooner she'd get past the pain and shame and get on with her life.

Giving up the pretense of sleep, she rose for good, directing her restless energy to the task of cleaning up the painful reminders of their brief intimacy, changing the sheets and pillowcases so that they no longer smelled like him. She picked up his discarded clothes and packed them away, along with the rest of his clothes, into the pair of large duffels he'd brought with him after he moved in.

He wouldn't need to be here after tonight's fundraiser, after all. He could go back to his real life—and let her and Zachary get on with theirs. Zachary wasn't going to be happy, of course, but she'd figure out some way to distract him until he settled into the idea of Harlan no longer being around.

At 6:00 a.m., she called Charlotte Manning to make sure she could still watch Zachary during the fundraiser, but once she heard her friend's gentle voice, she found herself blurting out the mistake she'd made the night before, giving in to the need to cry on her friend's shoulder. She didn't go into details, but Charlotte was a smart woman who easily read between the lines.

"Are you sure you have this right?" Charlotte asked after Stacy finished, her voice soft with sympathy and concern.

"How else am I supposed to read it?" Stacy dashed tears from her cheeks with angry jabs of her fingertips. "Not a note, not a goodbye, just slam, bam—"

"Come on, Stacy. He's in the middle of an intense security project. How do you know he didn't get called away for something related to the fundraiser?"

The surge of hope Charlotte's words evoked was almost embarrassing. "I thought about that, but it doesn't explain why he didn't at least leave me a note."

"I just think you should discuss it with him before you jump to any conclusions."

"There's nothing to discuss," Stacy said sharply. "Harlan and I both knew before we got ourselves into this mess that neither of us wanted anything serious. Anthony cured me of that kind of romanticism."

"And that's why you're crying your heart out over a one-night stand?" Charlotte's voice flattened. "Anthony hurt you, Stacy, but that doesn't mean Harlan—or some other guy—is going to do the same thing."

"I'm glad you can still believe in true love and happily ever after," Stacy said, meaning it. Maybe, if she were stronger and braver, if she didn't have Zachary's welfare and happiness to worry about, she'd be more willing to take a chance on something impossible.

But she couldn't take any more chances, especially after making the mistake of putting aside her lingering doubts last night and taking a leap of hope.

"Stacy, at least talk to him—"

"I have to go. You need to get ready for school, and Zachary will be up any minute." She said a quick goodbye and hung up before Charlotte tempted her good sense any further.

She woke Zachary and dressed him for school, expecting Harlan to walk through the door any moment with some lame excuse about where he'd gone and why he hadn't left her a note or called. She was ready for him, however—his bags were packed by the sofa and she was cleaned up and sobered up by cold, hard reality.

No tears. No arguments. No begging for any sort of reconsideration. And if she felt hurt or ashamed by her mistake last night, she'd be damned if she showed it.

But by the time she had to leave to take Zachary to school, Harlan still hadn't arrived or even called.

She wrote a quick note and tucked it under the canvas strap of one of the duffels, where he couldn't miss it.

Taking a final look at the bags sitting on the floor by the sofa, she followed Zachary out the front door.

JEFF ARRIVED HOME a little after 7:30 a.m., his grim expression making Harlan's gut twist with apprehension. Harlan didn't know the deputy well enough to know whether his grimace denoted finding something disturbing during the search of Trevor Lewis's apartment—or finding nothing at all.

The answer was both. Sort of.

"The sheriff doesn't think this is automatically actionable, by itself," Jeff explained in an apologetic tone, laying a manila envelope on the table in front of Harlan. "But it's not *nothing.*"

Harlan eyed the envelope, torn between anticipation and dread. Jeff pushed it toward him, giving silent assent to go ahead and take a look at what was inside.

Harlan opened the envelope flap and carefully emptied the contents onto the table surface. A small collection of eight-by-ten photographs lay in front of him.

"Sheriff Hale said it was okay to show them to you, since you're heading up the governor's shindig tonight," Jeff said.

Harlan flipped through the photographs, his stomach tightening with rage as he saw the subject matter. The photographs depicted the interior of a small but well-furnished bedroom. Big iron bed, expensive-looking bedding and curtains. A low, wide dresser with a mirror took up most of one wall. And on the dresser, filling almost every available inch of surface stood a series of framed photographs.

Photographs of Stacy Giordano.

"That sick son of a—"

"I know." Jeff Appleton nodded with understanding. "I don't know what law he's broken by doing that, but I don't see how we can just ignore it, either, especially after what happened at the ranch yesterday."

Harlan looked back through the photographs again, paying particular attention to the close-up shots of the framed images on the dresser. They were all clearly candid shots of Stacy, taken without her knowledge, save for an ominous-looking image near the end of the dresser. That photo had clearly been clipped from the Austin newspaper only a few short days ago.

The photo depicted Stacy, dressed in her grimy, rumpled business suit, her face bloodied and haggard. It had been snapped just after she'd freed the governor from the collapsed dais; Harlan remembered seeing it the day it came out in the paper. Her gaze fixed on something beyond the camera lens, she looked shell-shocked and tragically beautiful, but Harlan doubted, somehow, that the aesthetic appeal of the shot was what had compelled Trevor Lewis to clip it from the newspaper.

Harlan clenched his jaw so tightly it ached. "It may not be enough to take him into custody, but it's enough to give the governor cover to fire him."

Appleton nodded soberly. "The sheriff gave me permission to let you take these copies to the governor as evidence. I don't know if he's dangerous to Stacy or not, but it's not a risk I think anyone wants to take."

"What about his connection to Planet Justice?" Harlan asked. "Did you find anything incriminating?"

"Some literature. Some black bloc–style clothing in his closet. But those things aren't illegal, and we didn't find any bomb-making material anywhere in the apartment." Jeff shrugged. "That doesn't mean he's not the bomber, though. Maybe he wouldn't want explosives where he lived. That's a high-end apartment for someone who works as a stable hand. He's got to have income coming from somewhere else."

"His parents are wealthy," Harlan said. While he'd waited for Jeff Appleton to return from the search of Lewis's apartment, he'd heard from Vince Russo with more on Trevor Lewis's background. He came from a wealthy family in the San Mateo area, wealthy enough to indulge his love for horses by subsidizing his work as a stable groom without incurring any real hardship for themselves.

"If he has money, maybe he rents or owns another place where he keeps the explosives," Appleton suggested.

"CSI is already looking into his finances," Harlan assured him. He eyed the weary-looking deputy. "Are you done for the day or do you have to go in to work?"

"I'm done for now—I'm part of the sheriff's detail of extra officers you requested to back up your men at the fundraiser." Jeff stifled a yawn. "Charlotte Manning's going to be watching Zachary anyway, so she said she'd be happy to keep an eye on Abby for me." He glanced toward the hall to the bedroom. "I'd better get Abby up and go check her into school. Did she wake up at all?"

"No. She won't know you were ever gone." Harlan

couldn't help but think about Zachary when he said the words. He glanced at his watch and saw with alarm that it was after eight o'clock. Stacy would have taken Zachary to school a half hour ago. She was probably waiting for him in her office, wondering why the hell he'd bugged out on her.

He kind of hated to tell her what had been going on while she slept. If the sight of those photos creeped out Harlan, what would they do to Stacy?

Chapter Sixteen

Harlan stopped off at the guesthouse, planning to shower and re-dress. He held out a small hope that Stacy might have gone back home before heading into the office for the big day of last-minute preparations, but when he asked the guard on duty if he'd seen her, he told Harlan that Stacy had taken Zachary to school and hadn't returned.

Inside, he went to the hall closet to pull out fresh clothes for work but found nothing there but a few empty hangers. He shut the door, confused. Had she moved his clothes to her own closet? Was it her way of saying he was welcome in her bed for more than just one night?

But when he checked her closet, he found only her clothes. The clothes he'd shucked off last night were nowhere around.

He went back to the living room and found the answer to the mystery. His two duffel bags were sitting by the sofa, and if their shapes were anything to go by, all his clothes had been repacked inside. A folded piece of paper lay tucked under one of the duffel bag handles.

Apprehension making his gut clench, he opened the note. It was from Stacy, written in her neat, spare cursive. "Harlan, thanks for all your help. Zachary and I appreciate all you've done to keep us safe. With the fundraiser happening tonight, you'll be going back to your own place, so

I thought I'd go ahead and get your things together for you as a thank-you."

She'd signed her name at the bottom. No postscript, no mention of what had happened between them the night before.

It was as if she'd decided to erase him from her life.

She'd said she wasn't in the market for a relationship. He hadn't been, either, until he met her and couldn't get her out of his head.

After last night, he'd been sure she was beginning to feel the same way. In his arms, she'd been fierce and generous, taking everything he gave her and giving it right back to him. Could he have been wrong about what she was feeling?

Maybe her experience with her ex had done more of a number on her than he'd realized, he thought, refolding the note and tucking it into the pocket of his pants. If he ever ran into Anthony Giordano, he was going to have a hell of a lot to say.

Locking up behind him, he picked up the envelope full of photos he'd laid on the table by the door and headed outside. He left the truck parked in front of the guesthouse and walked the hundred yards between the guesthouse and the governor's sprawling villa. It took him halfway there before the obvious answer for Stacy's behavior slapped him right in the face.

He had left her bed without even leaving a note.

No phone calls to check in on her, no word at all. Just sex and a hasty escape—that's what it would have looked like to her, wouldn't it? No wonder she'd packed his bags and given him a brush-off note.

Stacy was in with the governor when Harlan knocked on the door. She looked up with cool lack of interest that made his chest ache. But he saw something in her eyes that convinced him she wasn't as indifferent as she was trying to appear. A hint of pain at the sight of him, giving him evidence that he'd been right. She thought he considered her a one-night stand.

He'd disabuse her of that notion as soon as he could, but first, he had to show her and the governor what the Freedom Sheriff's Department had found during their search of Trevor Lewis's apartment.

He pulled up the chair the governor gestured toward and put the manila envelope on the desk in front of him. Stacy slanted a curious look at the envelope, but Lila ignored it. "I hear the Freedom Sheriff's Department raided Trevor Lewis's apartment in the middle of the night. You have anything to do with that?"

Harlan glanced at Stacy. She didn't look surprised by the governor's words, so this wasn't the first she'd heard of it. Why was she still upset with him, if she knew why he'd left?

"I was tangentially involved," he answered, dragging his gaze away from Stacy's down-turned face.

"Did they find anything connecting him to the bombing in Austin?" Stacy asked, still not looking at him.

"No. But he's connected to Planet Justice, the group that's going to hold a protest tonight outside the fundraiser."

Stacy's gaze finally rose to meet his. "You're kidding."

He shook his head. "That's not the worst of it." He opened the envelope and pulled out the photos. "The deputies found this in his bedroom."

He watched as horrified realization spread over her face, wondering if he should have softened the blow somehow. Why had he just sprung the photos on her without any preparation?

Was he that desperate to make her look at him again?

"My God," she whispered.

Lila Lockhart held her hand out for the photos. Stacy

handed them to the governor, who slipped on her glasses and flipped through the photographs, her expression darkening.

"This may not be legally actionable evidence, but it's enough for me. I'll take my lumps and fire the creepy little SOB from the stables. If he wants to make a public stink, I'll tell them all about this bedroom shrine, and if he thinks I don't have the gumption to do it, he doesn't know who I am."

Harlan smiled at the governor's outburst. "Good. That's what I was hoping you'd say."

"He may end up at the protest anyway," Stacy pointed out in a quiet voice, still looking shocked and disturbed.

Harlan fought the urge to pull her into his arms and comfort her. At least, not here in front of the governor.

"Stacy, I'm done with you for now—go ahead and get to the last-minute tasks you were telling me about. And don't forget my hairdresser from Dallas will be here this afternoon to doll us up for the big shindig." Lila flashed her aide a dazzling smile before her expression grew sympathetic. "Try not to worry too much about those pictures. If Trevor Lewis so much as steps foot on this ranch, I'll make sure he's kicked off, pronto."

"Thank you," Stacy murmured and left the office.

Lila turned back to look at Harlan. "Looks like you've got your work cut out for you, Mr. McClain."

"Yes, ma'am, I know," he answered, aware that keeping peace at tonight's fundraiser was only half the battle he had to win.

"Will you do me a favor, Mr. McClain?" the governor added as he headed for the exit.

"Of course, Governor."

"Please have Mr. Cavanaugh with your agency give me a call. I have a project for him."

"Sure," he answered, heading down the hallway. He made

a mental note to call Nick as soon as he got back to his office.

But first, he had someone else he needed to see.

SHE'D GOTTEN THROUGH seeing Harlan okay, hadn't she?

Stacy gazed at her pale face in the mirror of her office bathroom, her haunted eyes accusing her of cowardice. She should be waiting in Harlan's office to confront him about leaving her bed without even a note, not hiding in her office like a scared teenager.

But confront him for what? For doing his job?

"Still could have left a note," she muttered aloud, but the gripe sounded petty in the face of the evidence the search warrant had unearthed.

Hearing footsteps outside, she dried her hands and left the bathroom to find Harlan standing just inside her office doorway.

He met her wary gaze with a look of sheer male intensity that made her insides quake and deliberately closed the door behind him. "Thanks for packing my bags."

Looked like she was getting the confrontation whether she wanted it or not. "I figured with the fundraiser tonight, you might not have a chance to pack yourself."

"Is that what you figured?" He stepped closer. "The danger won't be over tonight. Whoever set that bomb in Austin won't stop just because the party is over."

"But the direct danger to me was getting the crank phone calls. And the flower on my porch—and clearly, that had to be Trevor, don't you think?" She edged away from him, unnerved not by his nearness but by her nearly uncontrollable reaction to him. She felt a sensation low in her belly that was almost like a craving, a deep pang of need threatening to swamp her struggling self-control.

Last night, his lovemaking had been tender but demanding, pushing her to places, both physically and emotionally, that she'd never gone before, and her body seemed unwilling to walk away from that kind of experience unchanged, even if her mind was fighting hard to pretend it had been nothing but two bodies coming together to do what two bodies were created to do.

"You're just coming up with excuses to make me go away," he said in a low, sexy growl that made her bones melt. "I thought we were past that point in our relationship."

She stepped away farther, turning to the window so she wouldn't have to look at him. Outside, the long veranda was a hive of activity, workmen putting last-minute touches on the decorations on the ranch house's exterior. "We don't have a relationship," she said aloud. "Until the party is over, you're sort of my boss, I suppose. But that ends tonight."

"So last night was, what? Scratching an itch?"

She grimaced at his hard words. "I guess."

"I slept with you, Stacy."

"Not for long."

"And that's the problem, right? I got up and left your bed without waking you?"

She forced herself to face him. "That's pretty much always a problem for a woman, you know, waking to find the man she just had sex with couldn't stick around for the cuddling phase."

He arched his eyebrows. "We cuddled. Damned good cuddling, as I recall."

He was trying to make her laugh now, she realized, as if he could cajole her into seeing everything his way. Anthony used to do that, and she used to let him. "Stop. Please."

He released a frustrated sigh. "Tell me what you want from me. An apology? I'm sorry. I shouldn't have tried to keep you out of what was going on. I should have awakened you, or at least left you a note about where I was going."

She wanted to accept his apology, wanted it so much it felt like a fire burning in her belly. But what would forgiveness solve? Was she just going to fall into another disastrous relationship because he was charming and strong and great in bed? That's what had happened with Anthony.

"I think we should forget last night ever happened. After the party tonight, there's no reason we should see much of each other again." Even as she said the words aloud, a hard pain settled in the center of her chest, making her queasy.

"So that's it. You're done."

She nodded. "I'm done."

He released a long, slow breath. "Okay." She heard him walk toward the door, then stop. She looked up as he turned around to look at her again. "Can I tell Zachary goodbye?"

The look in Harlan's eyes was impossible to resist. "Okay. Tonight, before the fundraiser, you can come say goodbye."

Harlan nodded. "Thank you."

Then he was gone.

She lifted shaking hands to her face, pushing her hair away from her forehead. Tears hammered her eyes but she forced them to stay put. She wasn't going to fall apart today. She'd made a decision, and she was strong enough to live with it.

All she had to do was get through this fundraiser and it would all be over.

WHEN HARLAN STOPPED BY the guesthouse later that afternoon, he already knew he wasn't going to see Stacy. He'd spotted her thirty minutes ago, walking into the office area carrying a vinyl dress bag. Apparently she was going to get ready for the party at the main house.

He'd already donned his tuxedo during a quick trip home to his apartment for a shave and a shower. Zachary made a face when he spotted Harlan coming through the door. "You look like you're going to a funeral," Zachary commented. "Are you?"

He'd have about as much fun at a funeral, Harlan thought. He sat on the coffee table across from Zachary's perch on the sofa. "No, just a party."

"So's Mommy. Are you going to the party with her?"

"We'll both be at the party," Harlan answered carefully.

"Will you and Mommy bring me cake from the party?"

"I'll ask your mama for you."

"You could bring it."

Harlan slanted a quick glance at Charlotte Manning, who was watching them from the kitchen. He saw in her eyes a look of knowing sadness that convinced him Stacy had warned her why he'd be stopping by. He supposed Charlotte would need to be in the loop, since she'd have to spend the rest of the night with Zachary once the goodbyes were said.

He looked back at Zachary. "I won't be coming back, Zachary. My job is over tonight, and you and your mama will have the place to yourselves again."

Zachary looked puzzled. "But you moved in."

"Only for a little while. I have to go back to my own place. My furniture misses me. Just like the horses miss you when you don't go ride."

"You can come see me ride, right? Your furniture can let you come see me ride."

Harlan's heart felt as if it had ripped in two, pain bleeding into his chest. "I'll talk to your mama about that." He reached out and smoothed a spiky strand of hair on Zachary's head. The child didn't flinch, a sign of his trust in Harlan. "Listen here, Zachary, I'm going to ask you to do something for me, okay? It's real important."

Zachary nodded. "Okay."

"I want you to take real good care of your mama. You watch after her and be real good to her, for me."

"Okay," Zachary answered solemnly.

"And if either one of you ever need anything, you ask for me, okay? 'Cause I'll come running if you need me."

Zachary nodded again. "You'll come running."

Harlan reached across and pulled the little boy into a fierce hug. After a couple of seconds, Zachary started struggling.

"One, two, three, let go!" he said indignantly.

Harlan let him go. "Sorry. Next time I'll count." He headed for the door before he started doing something embarrassing, such as blubbering like a baby.

He turned in the doorway to get one last look at Zachary. The little boy had already lost interest in Harlan, taking his goodbye at face value, and was playing with a couple of toy horses on the coffee table.

But Charlotte Manning was watching him with shining eyes. He gave her a quick nod goodbye and left the house, trotting down the porch steps before he changed his mind and went back.

With each step he took up the path to the main house, he felt as if he was leaving behind the only life that would ever make him happy.

STACY STRAIGHTENED HER DRESS and took a deep breath before stepping out of the governor's personal library onto the open gallery that circled the ballroom one story below. Guests had started arriving a few minutes ago, but she still had time to make a quick run down to the guesthouse to check on Zachary and Charlotte before the fundraiser went into full swing.

Unfortunately, the ground rules Harlan had set stated that any staffer leaving the main house had to check in with him first so he could alert the perimeter guards.

She found him only a few feet down the gallery, standing at the balcony that overlooked the main floor. The spacious ballroom was the one interior room that looked as if it belonged within the Italianate villa exterior of the Twin Harts ranch house. Oval-shaped, flanked by eight tall white columns supporting the open gallery on the second floor and decorated in neutral shades of white, cream, gold and peach, the ballroom looked like something out of an old movie.

About twenty early arrivals milled about the ballroom, chatting and enjoying the champagne and hors d'oeuvres several white-jacketed waiters offered on shiny silver trays.

Like the rest of the security agents, Harlan was dressed in a simple black tuxedo with a necktie in lieu of a more formal bow tie. He'd shaved since she'd spotted him on her way into the ranch house earlier that afternoon. In fact, he looked completely edible, and she didn't know how she was going to get through the rest of the night without making a fool of herself.

He turned at her approach, his eyes darkening with a pure, feral hunger that seemed to match her own. "Stacy."

She swallowed hard. "Just the man I was looking for."

She saw a flicker of hope in his eyes and realized he thought she had sought him out for personal reasons.

She hadn't, had she?

"I need clearance from you to leave the ranch house," she said aloud. "I want to run down to check on Zachary and Charlotte before the party gets into full swing."

"Why don't I get one of the agents to walk you over there?" he asked, looking uneasy.

"It's not necessary," she said.

He lowered his voice. "The danger isn't over yet, Stacy. Don't let anything that went on between the two of us make you forget that."

"I haven't." She softened her voice. "I appreciate your concern about me. And Zachary."

He leaned closer. "When this party's over, I want to talk to you. Can I come over tonight?"

Temptation burned low in her belly. But she forced herself to shake her head. "Not a good idea."

"Then tomorrow. Let me come by tomorrow."

"Harlan—" She could feel herself crumbling, and it scared her to death.

"Okay. I'll call ahead and let them know you're coming."

She started to walk away, then turned to look at him, unable to cut herself off from him completely. "Maybe we could have coffee at Talk of the Town in a couple of days."

That was noncommittal, wasn't it? She could change her mind if she wanted to.

He smiled. "That sounds good. You have my number."

She returned the smile tentatively and escaped downstairs, her cheeks burning. Greeting a few of the early arriving guests, she weaved her way to the side exit and stopped there for a moment, looking back at the second floor gallery.

Harlan still stood at the railing, watching her.

Her face burning, she headed outside into the cool night.

She knew Jeff Appleton was the agent guarding the checkpoint outside the guesthouse, since he'd asked Charlotte to watch Abby along with Zachary. But he wasn't at his post when she reached the checkpoint.

Had he gone into the house to check on Abby? A breach of security protocol like that didn't sound much like Jeff, but he was pretty crazy about his kid.

She'd left her keys back at the ranch house, locked in Lila's office, so she knocked on the door and waited for Charlotte to answer.

But it wasn't Charlotte Manning who opened the door.

It was Trevor Lewis.

"UNIT SEVEN TO UNIT ONE. We need backup!" Vince Russo's voice barked in Harlan's ear as he watched the governor readying herself to climb the shallow steps of the riser holding a delicate brass podium from which she'd speak in a minute or two.

"Unit Seven, what's the situation?" He stepped back into an alcove, not wanting to raise alarm among the guests gathered on the ballroom floor.

"Black bloc action on the protest front. They're overrunning the perimeter guards. We need at least three or four more bodies to get them back in line!"

Harlan radioed the other checkpoints that had multiple guards and peeled off three agents to head for the south gate, where the governor had provided a cordoned-off protest area.

He kept a close eye on the ballroom as he did so, not liking the timing of the sudden eruption from the protestors. He couldn't pour all his attention and resources into quelling the protestors—they could be a decoy designed to draw his attention away from the governor.

He headed toward the governor. "Ma'am, we have a situation." He told her what was happening. "I think we need to consider evacuating the guests from the ballroom."

"Surely you're overreacting—"

"Harlan!" A high-pitched, unmistakable voice rose over the murmur of the crowd, drawing Harlan's attention away from the governor. He scanned the crowd for a face he knew couldn't possibly be there.

But there he was, only a few yards away, looking tiny and rumpled in his pajamas with the yellow ponies galloping over a blue field. Zachary spotted Harlan and crossed the floor as fast as his slipper-clad feet would take him.

"Unit Two, Unit Six, cover Cowgirl," Harlan said into the headset, referring to the governor, as he hurried to meet

Zachary halfway. The fear in the boy's eyes made his gut twist.

"You said to find you if Mommy needed you," Zachary said, out of breath. "I ran all the way here to look for you."

"Where's your mama?"

"At home. You have to come."

Three fast cracking noises split the air. Around them, people started screaming and running.

Gunfire.

Chapter Seventeen

Curling himself around Zachary to keep the child from being hit by gunfire or trampled by the crowd, Harlan located the governor's position. Parker McKenna was blocking her body with his, while Nolan Law was covering Bart Bellows in his wheelchair as the agents hustled them both out the side exit, probably to the armored SUV parked outside for just such a contingency.

Relieved on one point, Harlan scanned the gallery above. The shots had come from that direction.

There. He saw movement behind one of the columns. A man dressed in all black, his face covered with a ski mask.

"All units, gunman on the second floor gallery, west section." He picked Zachary up and carried him beneath the overhang created by the second floor walkway, below the gunman's position. A doorway nearby led into the governor's office. He dug the keys to the office from his pocket and took Zachary inside. "Zachary, listen—you know how important promises are, right?"

Zachary was crying, but he nodded.

"Promise you'll stay here until I come get you. Promise?"

Zachary nodded again.

Zachary kissed the little boy's forehead. "I love you, little man. Stay right here and I'll be back to get you. I promise."

"Promises are important," Zachary said on a soft hitching sob.

"That's right." Harlan slipped out the door on the opposite side of the office, locking it behind him.

Listening to the radio chatter to get his bearings, he tried to anticipate where the gunman might go now that he'd been thwarted in his quest to shoot the governor. But all he could think about was what Zachary had said to him just before the shots rang out. *You said to find you if Mommy needed you.*

When was the last time he'd seen Stacy? When she headed to the guesthouse to check on Zachary and the others?

"Unit Ten, this is Unit One." Unit Ten was Jeff Appleton, the deputy in charge of guarding the guesthouse. He'd talked to Appleton right before Stacy left so he'd know she was coming.

Had he talked to him since?"

"Unit Ten, please respond."

Nothing.

Fear settled in the center of Harlan's chest, heavy as lead. "Unit Seven, Unit Ten is not responding."

"Unit One, can't check. All hell's broken loose out here."

"All units, Unit One going to check on Unit Ten. Keep looking for the gunman."

He headed for the side exit, keeping an eye out for the gunman who'd opened fire in the hall. Panicked guests were being herded out of the ballroom doors a few yards to the north, while other security units were scouring the ranch house in search of the shooter.

How the hell had the man in black gotten past the checkpoints to get inside? They had metal detectors set up at all the main entrances—any weapon should have been caught on the scan.

He set that question aside and concentrated on making

a quiet approach toward the checkpoint outside the guesthouse. It was empty, he saw to his surprise, but he heard a soft moaning sound coming from somewhere to his left.

Sidetracking, he nearly stumbled over something lying on the shadowy ground beneath a tall cottonwood tree. Flashing the penlight on his key ring onto the ground, he saw Jeff Appleton lying on his side, bleeding from his head. His eyes were fluttering, as if he was trying to regain consciousness.

His sidearm was missing.

"Appleton, it's McClain." Harlan crouched by the man, scanning the area to make sure he wasn't being lured into an ambush. There were no strange sounds, no sign of any furtive movements around him. "Can you hear me?"

Appleton's eyes flickered open. "McClain." He winced, touching his hand to his bleeding head.

"Who hit you?"

"Got me from behind." He blinked hard and tried to sit up, groaning at the effort.

"Don't move—I'll call for a medical unit."

"Wait." Appleton grabbed Harlan's arm. "Trevor Lewis."

Harlan frowned at him. "What about Lewis?"

"Before I got knocked out, I spotted Lewis heading for the house. It was just after you radioed me to tell me Stacy was coming." His grip on Harlan's arm weakened. "He had...a key...." His eyes fluttered shut. He was still breathing and still had a strong, steady pulse, Harlan saw with relief. He eased the man to the ground and radioed in his position.

"Unit Ten is down. Need medical assistance." His gaze slid to the quiet facade of Stacy's home, his heart pounding a cadence of pure terror. "We may have a hostage situation at the guesthouse."

"What do you want?" Stacy fought to keep her voice low and calm, even though panic screamed through every cell of her body. Where was Zachary? She'd seen him for a split second when she came into the house, before Trevor locked her son and Jeff Appleton's little girl, Abby, in Zachary's bedroom and told them to stay there.

She'd heard Abby crying inconsolably off and on for the past half hour, but not a peep from Zachary.

How would a kid with Asperger's react to something this unexpected and strange? Shut down and pretend it wasn't happening? It was possible.

She hoped that was the answer. If he shut down, then maybe he wasn't living through the terror that poor Abby Appleton seemed to be experiencing at the moment, her cries rising from inside the locked bedroom.

Trevor sat on one of the bar stools, his posture almost relaxed, though the pistol he held pointed at Charlotte's bound, gagged figure belied any sort of calm on his part. "I'm waiting for the signal."

"What signal?"

"I'll know it when I hear it. Then we can get Zachary and go." He shot a look at Charlotte, who was gazing at him with wide, terrified eyes. "I'm not going to hurt you if everyone just cooperates. I just came for Stacy, but we have to wait for the signal before we can go."

"What about Deputy Appleton? What did you do to get past him?" Stacy asked.

"*I* didn't do anything," Trevor answered, but the emphasis he put on the first word provided a frightening clue. If he hadn't done anything to Jeff, did he have an accomplice who had?

"Where do you plan to take Zachary and me?" she asked aloud.

"Did you know my family has money?" Trevor smiled at her. "Lots of it. I got the bulk of an inheritance from my grandfather when I turned twenty-five. Last year, I bought a small horse ranch in Colorado. You and Zachary will love it there. He'll have horses to ride whenever he wants to, and you can stop worrying so hard about making ends meet." Trevor rose from the chair and crossed to where she sat on the sofa. He sank onto the coffee table, reaching across to touch her cheek. "I just want to take care of both of you. You haven't had anyone to do that for you since your husband left, have you?"

A picture of Harlan flashed in her head. Strong, solid Harlan, who loved her son and seemed to want more from her than she was brave enough to give him. He'd take care of her and Zachary, if she needed him to, but he respected her ability to take care of herself and her son on her own.

The comparison to the crazy man sitting in front of her with his gun still held at the ready was enough to bring stinging tears to her eyes. But she held them back, refusing to let the fear make her weaker.

Harlan would realize she hadn't returned to the party, sooner or later. He knew where she'd been going when she left the ranch house. He'd come looking.

She just had to stay alert, listen for signs of his arrival. If she could distract Trevor at just the right time—

"Zachary's being awfully quiet." Trevor pushed himself to his feet, reaching down to catch her wrist. "Let's go check."

She shook her head, not wanting her son to see her being held at gunpoint. "You know Zachary. He's probably caught up in reading one of his horse books."

"He's probably hungry, don't you think?" He glanced at the counter, where the half-eaten remains of vegetable soup sat cooling in bowls. "I interrupted dinner, I'm afraid."

He dragged her down the hall to Zachary's bedroom, untying the shoestrings he'd used to secure the door closed by tying it to Stacy's bedroom doorknob. At the rattle of the doorknob, Abby Appleton started crying again.

Trevor opened the door. Abby sobbed in terror.

But Stacy didn't see Zachary.

"Where is he?" Trevor asked the crying child.

She just sobbed harder.

"Ask her!" Trevor's grip tightened on Stacy's arm, pushing her into the room.

She stumbled forward, almost falling into the crying child. Catching herself, she crouched by Abby, reaching out to touch the child's cold, damp cheek. "Abby, where did Zachary go?"

Abby's blue eyes shifted sideways.

Toward the open bedroom window.

"WE HAVE MOVEMENT INSIDE." Around the side of the house, Freedom Sheriff Bernard Hale motioned for Harlan to join him. Behind them, EMTs had arrived, lights and sirens off, to make sure no one inside the ranch house was alerted to the police presence. They scooped up Appleton and carried him off to a safer staging area closer to the road.

Back at the ranch house, the agents had finished a thorough sweep without finding the mysterious gunman who'd fired shots at the governor earlier. They had, however, found a gun hidden in a plant in the upper gallery. It had been recently fired.

Matt Soarez was staying with Zachary in the governor's office until Harlan could get back to the house. Zachary refused to leave until Harlan came back to get him.

Harlan scooted closer to the sheriff. They were looking through the open window of Zachary's bedroom, he realized. That's how the little boy had gotten out.

Borrowing the sheriff's binoculars, he peered into the room and saw Trevor Lewis standing at the window, looking out.

"It's Lewis," he confirmed in a low whisper. He and the sheriff were pretty well camouflaged by the scrubby bush giving them cover, but he still hunched lower as Trevor looked out the window briefly before ducking inside. "Wish I had my M40."

"You're a sniper?" Hale asked.

"Used to be," he answered. Of course, it had been a while since he'd been able to shoot a rifle with any sort of confidence. The man at the firing range thought it was more mental than physical for Harlan, but based on what the doctors had told him when he'd first sustained the injury, the scar tissue alone would preclude regaining his old form.

"I can get you a Remington M24."

"Shouldn't we try negotiating first?" Harlan asked.

"Of course," Hale answered. "Just thinking about contingencies." He thumbed the radio on his shoulder. "All units, hold position. I'm going to make a call." He looked at Harlan. "I need the number."

Harlan rattled it off, keeping his eye on the window. He couldn't see Lewis anymore, but he caught a glimpse of a curvy silhouette against a rectangle of light inside the room. Stacy, he thought, his heart in his throat

"Stacy's in there with him," he said to Hale.

"You sure?"

He nodded. He'd know the shape of her anywhere.

Hale dialed the number, his cell phone on speaker. The phone inside rang four times before Stacy answered. "Hello?"

She sounded scared, Harlan thought. And brave. A surge of emotion racked him, as if someone had opened a floodgate inside and let the pent-up energy flow.

He loved her. Everything about her, from her bloody stubborn streak to her blasted pride. And if it was the last thing he ever did, he'd get her out of that house safely and reunite her with that quirky little kid they both loved so much.

"STACY, THIS IS BERNARD HALE." The sheriff's voice came over the line loud and clear, as if he were in the next room. That meant he was probably somewhere close, maybe just outside. "Is Trevor Lewis in there with you?"

Stacy flinched as Trevor rested his chin on her shoulder from behind, his ear pressing the phone receiver against her own ear. "He's right here."

"I'd like to speak to him."

Trevor's hot breath brushed her cheek. "Tell him no." He backed away, pacing a few steps toward the kitchen. "See what your kid did? Sneaked out and made trouble for us. Maybe if you didn't baby him so much, he wouldn't have bugged out."

Trevor was losing it, she thought, trying not to let the gnawing panic in her belly take hold. "It's not too late to stop this," she said to Trevor, pleased that her voice remained calm and even despite the fear.

"He'll stop it," Trevor said with manic confidence. "He has a plan."

"Who's 'he'?" she asked, hoping the sheriff was taking notes on the other end of the line.

"You'll find out soon enough," Trevor murmured, his voice almost gleeful.

"Stacy, it's Harlan." The low-pitched, familiar voice in her ear set her nerves jangling. "Is he listening in now?"

"No," she murmured.

"Yes, you will," Trevor said, waving the gun in a wide sweep. "He's got it all worked out."

"Zachary's okay," Harlan said. "He came to get me."

Her heart leaped. "Really?"

Trevor gave her an odd look. "Yes. Are you willing to be part of it, too?"

"Jeff Appleton's injured but being treated. Are Charlotte and his daughter okay?"

"Yes," she answered.

Trevor's eyes lit up. "Really?"

In her ear, Harlan gave her a quick update. "A gunman shot at the governor. She's okay. Nobody hurt, just bumps and bruises for the guests during the evacuation." His voice was a bracing shot of whiskey, shoring up her flagging strength. "We didn't catch the shooter, but he's long gone."

So Trevor's dream of some big plan unfolding wasn't going to come true. But would sharing that information with her unstable captor make things better or worse? At this point, he seemed to have lost all touch with reality and didn't even notice she was still on the phone.

"I'm willing to be part of it," she said aloud to Trevor. "But I don't think we should depend on someone else. Why can't we just come up with our own plan?"

"I need to know where you are. We don't have a bead on the guy," Harlan murmured.

She met Trevor's beaming gaze, wondering how to reveal their position without tipping him off. If she could keep Trevor from getting shot, that's what she wanted to do. But the more he waved around that gun, the sooner someone was going to get hurt. She didn't intend for it to be Charlotte, Abby or her. "Trevor, why don't you untie Charlotte and let her go? She can take Abby with her. They'll tell Sheriff Hale that everything's okay—won't you Charlotte?"

Charlotte nodded, her eyes dark with desperation.

"See?"

Trevor shook his head. "You don't believe her, do you?" He raised the gun and pointed it right at Charlotte's head. Charlotte flinched, squeezing her eyes shut.

"No!" Stacy took a step toward him, keeping the phone pressed to her ear so she didn't lose the connection to Harlan. "I believe her. I do. She's my best friend. She'd do anything to protect me. She's not going to let me get in trouble for helping you."

Trevor lowered the gun. "She may not, but nobody out there is going to believe her. Harlan McClain will poison their minds against me."

"Tell him to trade Charlotte and Abby for me," Harlan urged in her ear.

"No," she said sharply, seeing the black fury in Trevor's eyes. She had no doubt that if Harlan stepped foot inside the house right now, Trevor would shoot him dead on the spot.

"He will," Trevor insisted, pointing the gun at Charlotte again. The anger in his eyes melted into bleakness. "We're not getting out of here alive, Stacy. They won't let us. We're surrounded and he's not coming, is he?"

"Maybe your friend's just not here yet," she said quickly, not liking the look in his eyes. "Maybe he's looking for a distraction—if we could send out Charlotte and Abby, the people outside would be so busy dealing with them—"

"He could make his move," Trevor finished for her, looking at her with almost childlike hope.

"Let me untie Charlotte. She could go get Abby."

"Is Abby in Zachary's room?" Harlan's voice was a low rumble in her ear.

"It's probably getting cold in Zachary's room for Abby, with the window open," she said to Trevor.

"We'll put someone at the window to get them out that way—just warn us if Trevor's coming with her," Harlan said.

Trevor looked at Stacy uncertainly. "You think it'll work?"

I hope so, she thought.

HARLAN HEARD A LOW THUD, and seconds later, the sound of ripping tape. Lewis must've duct-taped Charlotte Manning to a chair in the kitchen earlier "Stacy?" he murmured, needing to hear the sound of her voice. But she didn't answer.

"She probably put the phone down to unbind Charlotte," Sheriff Hale said softly, his gaze on the pair of tactical officers he'd just positioned on either side of Zachary's bedroom window. As long as Charlotte entered alone, they'd draw her and Jeff Appleton's daughter to the window and help them escape.

"There. Let Charlotte go get Abby." Stacy's voice was back in his ear again. He felt the tension in his gut ease.

"Good," he said. "Keep him from going with them."

"No, she can do it by herself," Stacy said, clearly talking to Trevor. "We need to stay here and figure out what we're going to do when your friend makes his move."

That's my girl, he thought. And he was going to do whatever it took to make her see they were right together as soon as he got her out of there.

A rectangle of light appeared in Zachary's room. The door opened and Harlan spotted Charlotte Manning's silhouette enter.

The men at the window called softly to her. Following their orders, she handed Abby out the window to one of them and let the other officer help her out. The deputies brought Abby and Charlotte over to where Harlan and the sheriff crouched.

"Where are they?" Harlan asked Charlotte.

"Living room. He's going to come looking for me if I don't go back out there."

Sheriff Hale nodded to another deputy standing nearby. "That's what I'm counting on."

Charlotte looked at Harlan. "He's completely out of it— Stacy's walking around talking into the phone and it's like he doesn't even see it. You've got to get her out of there."

The deputy walked over, carrying an M24 police sniper rifle. He held it out to Harlan.

Harlan stared at the rifle, realizing what Hale intended. "Sheriff, no—"

On the other end of his headset, he heard Stacy's soft intake of breath.

"Everything's okay," he murmured into the microphone.

"You said you were a sniper," Hale said.

"I have an injury." He held up his shrapnel-scarred hand.

"What's taking so long?" Trevor Lewis's agitated voice was clear over the line. He must be standing close to Stacy.

Harlan realized they were out of time. Lewis seemed to be growing more desperate by the second, and now Stacy was the only remaining target for his madness. He had to end this mess.

Now.

It had been too long since he'd felt as if a sniper rifle was part of his own body, a third arm with which he could deliver justice in a few well-aimed and well-considered shots. But if that was the only way to make sure Stacy got a chance to hold her little boy again, then he'd make it happen.

He held out his hand to the deputy with the rifle. Into the headset, he murmured, "Get him into Zachary's room, turn on the light, and get the hell out of the way."

On the other end of the line, Stacy was silent for a long moment. Then, aloud, she said, "We should go check on them."

Harlan positioned himself for the best possible shot through the open window. His heart was rattling like a snare drum, beating a cadence of fear, but he shook off the doubt and concentrated on the task. Level the sight. Go for center mass.

A silhouette filled the doorway of Zachary's room, blocking part of the light. Harlan had the shot, but he didn't know where Stacy was, so he couldn't take it yet.

"They're not here." Trevor's voice rose with alarm. Harlan could hear him both on the headset and faintly through the open window twenty yards away.

"Are you sure?" Stacy's voice was strong over the line. "Let me turn on a light."

Harlan saw her silhouette just behind Trevor's. Her arm moved, flicking on the light in Zachary's room.

Illumination flooded the shadowy scene. Harlan saw Trevor Lewis clearly, standing a few feet inside the room. Behind him, Stacy backed out of Zachary's room at a run.

Trevor turned and ran to the doorway. His gun hand lifted, as if to fire after his escaping captive. Harlan heard a bark of gunfire from the house.

Now or never. Take the shot.

Hoping the short distance would compensate for the unfamiliar rifle and his rusty skills, he squeezed off three shots. Trevor Lewis's body jerked with each round.

Then he fell out of sight.

For a second, only the sound of the rifle's echo filled the night air. Then the area erupted in chaos as deputies and agents rushed the guesthouse.

Harlan handed off the rifle and ran to the front of the house, terrified that Lewis's round had hit its target before Harlan's shots took him down. He pushed past the deputies in the front room, calling Stacy's name.

"Harlan!" Her cry swung him in the direction of the kitchen, where she was standing near the sink, tears streaming down her eyes.

Elbowing deputies and agents out of the way, he ran to her, wrapping her in a crushing embrace. Her breath hot and sweet against his cheek, she whispered, "I knew you'd come."

He kissed her temple. "I always will."

Epilogue

The silence in Harlan's apartment was unnerving. Even though Stacy knew there was a guard posted outside to protect her and Zachary, she didn't feel safe.

Not until Harlan finally came home.

He looked tired when he came through the door. Tired and a little haunted. After Harlan put him in charge of taking her and Zachary back to his apartment and posting a guard while he briefed the other CSI agents at the office, Matt Soarez had told Stacy what Harlan had kept from her: shooting Trevor Lewis had been the shot of a lifetime for Harlan, given the injury to his hand. Doctors had told him he'd never be able to shoot a rifle for accuracy again. It was a big damned deal.

But why hadn't Harlan told her that? Why did she have to learn everything important about Harlan from other people?

"Zachary asleep?" he asked, shrugging off his overcoat to reveal his rumpled tuxedo. The tie was untied, hanging loose at the collar, and grime marred the snowy surface of his shirt.

"Yeah." She wanted to be strong, not let her feelings show. Not until she knew he meant those words he'd whispered in her ear when he'd come into the chaotic crime scene to find her. She couldn't deny she loved him, but she had to be sure she was making the right choices for Zachary and herself.

She'd loved Anthony, and look where that had gotten her.

"Any luck finding the gunman?"

Harlan shook his head. "We think he worked with Trevor Lewis to gain access to the ranch. I think Lewis had already planted the gun days ago so the man could sneak through the metal detector. The caterers had a man call in sick and hired a new guy without time to do much of a background check. We've got a description, but it's pretty vague. But we're still looking." He crossed to where she sat curled up on his sofa. "I'm sorry."

"Sorry about what?" she asked carefully.

There was almost no furniture in the room besides the sofa, not even a chair to pull up beside her. So he tugged the low coffee table forward and sat in front of her.

"That I had to deal with so much stuff before I could get back here to you." He reached across the distance between them and tucked a lock of her hair behind her ears, the touch light but warm. He let his fingers slide slowly down the side of her face, until his hand came to rest on her shoulder, his thumb gently stroking her collarbone. "That I left in the middle of the night last night and didn't get to wake up with you."

Damn it. Why was it so impossible to stay angry with him?

"You could have left a note." She tried not to get emotional, but after the day and night she'd just had, it would take a much harder woman than she to keep from feeling a little teary-eyed. "I mean, it was the first time we—"

He brushed his thumb across her trembling lower lip. "But not the last. Right?"

"You're such a man."

He grinned at her. "I'm afraid so."

She released a soft sigh, knowing she loved him anyway. "I guess you *were* kind of busy."

He eased off the coffee table and onto the sofa beside her, laying his arm across the back of the cushions. "When I got the call about Lewis, I had to go take care of it right then. And I know, I should have written a note, but all I thought about was getting Trevor out of the way so you and Zachary would be safe."

With another little sigh, she snuggled closer to him. "You've got this whole apology thing all figured out, don't you? Appeal to my concern for my son, snuggle up and make me feel warm and safe—you're really pretty ruthless, Mr. McClain."

He chuckled, the sound rumbling through her where their bodies touched. "I prefer the word *determined*."

"Determined to do what?" She gave him a look of challenge.

"This." He dipped his head, claiming her mouth with fierce intensity that had her head swimming in record time.

When he let her up for air a little later, she had forgotten why she'd ever been upset in the first place, although one sticking point came back a couple of minutes later, when Harlan was nuzzling the side of her neck. "You should have told me what a big deal it was to shoot a sniper rifle again."

He drew back to look at her. "I wasn't sure I could do it. It used to be as easy as breathing, but there was so much on the line tonight…."

The haggard look in his eyes did more to dispel the last of her doubts than anything he'd said. She rose to kiss him, hoping her touch would chase away his demons. He wrapped his arms around her, pulling her closer until she was sitting in his lap.

He caught her face between his hands, holding her as if she were a treasure he would never relinquish. "You know I can't let you go. Don't you?"

A bubble of joy popped in the center of her chest, spreading its warmth. "I know. I can't let you go, either. I thought it would make me feel weak and stupid to love you, but it doesn't."

He smiled at her, the expression taking years off his time-weathered face. "I love you, too. And I love that quirky, brilliant, amazing kid of yours, too."

She nuzzled her forehead against his chin. "Good thing, 'cause we're a package deal."

"Wouldn't have it any other way."

She wrapped her arms around his neck, bending in for another kiss. But before their lips touched, a plaintive voice spoke from the doorway.

"Will the horses know where to find me if I'm here?"

Stacy pulled away from Harlan and looked at her son, who stood in the doorway in his rumpled pajamas, his dark hair sticking up all over his sleepy head. She motioned for him to join them, sliding off Harlan's lap so Zachary could sit there.

Zachary climbed onto Harlan's lap, grinning up at him briefly before his expression went sober and worried again. "Can they find us? What if they think I've gone away forever?"

"They know where you are," Harlan assured him, running his hand down Zachary's back in a comforting caress. "Your mama and I told them personally."

Zachary leaned his sleepy head against Harlan's shoulder. The sight made Stacy's heart liquefy. "Okay, then."

Harlan looked at Stacy over the drowsy boy's head. "We have to tell the horses where he is tomorrow," he mouthed.

Happier than she could ever remember being, Stacy nodded and cuddled up to the two most important men in her life.

*****

DADDY CORPS *continues next month with*
CAMOUFLAGE COWBOY
by Jan Hambright,
wherever Harlequin Intrigue books are sold!

Harlequin®

INTRIGUE

COMING NEXT MONTH

Available November 8, 2011

#1311 CAMOUFLAGE COWBOY
Daddy Corps
Jan Hambright

#1312 SECRET PROTECTOR
Situation: Christmas
Ann Voss Peterson

#1313 DECODED
Colby Agency: Secrets
Debra Webb

#1314 GRAYSON
The Lawmen of Silver Creek Ranch
Delores Fossen

#1315 WESTIN FAMILY TIES
Open Sky Ranch
Alice Sharpe

#1316 WINTER HAWK'S LEGEND
Copper Canyon
Aimée Thurlo

You can find more information on upcoming
Harlequin® titles, free excerpts and more at
www.HarlequinInsideRomance.com.

---

*Harlequin® Special Edition® is thrilled to present a new
installment in* USA TODAY *bestselling author
RaeAnne Thayne's reader-favorite miniseries,*
THE COWBOYS OF COLD CREEK.

*Join the excitement as we meet the Bowmans—four
siblings who lost their parents but keep family ties alive
in Pine Gulch. First up is Trace. Only two things get under
this rugged lawman's skin: beautiful women and secrets.
And in Rebecca Parsons, he finds both!*

Read on for a sneak peek of
CHRISTMAS IN COLD CREEK.
Available November 2011 from Harlequin® Special Edition®.

On impulse, he unfolded himself from the bar stool. "Need
a hand?"

"Thank you! I…" She lifted her gaze from the floor to
his jeans and then raised her eyes. When she identified him
her hazel eyes turned from grateful to unfriendly and cold,
as if he'd somehow thrown the broken glasses at her head.

He also thought he saw a glimmer of panic in those
interesting depths, which instantly stirred his curiosity like
cream swirling through coffee.

"I've got it, Officer. Thank you." Her voice was several
degrees colder than the whirl of sleet outside the windows.

Despite her protests, he knelt down beside her and began
to pick up shards of broken glass. "No problem. Those trays
can be slippery."

This close, he picked up the scent of her, something fresh
and flowery that made him think of a mountain meadow on
a July afternoon. She had a soft, lush mouth and for one
brief, insane moment, he wanted to push aside that stray lock

of hair slipping from her ponytail and taste her. Apparently he needed to spend a lot less time working and a great deal *more* time recreating with the opposite sex if he could have sudden random fantasies about a woman he wasn't even inclined to like, pretty or not.

"I'm Trace Bowman. You must be new in town."

She didn't answer immediately and he could almost see the wheels turning in her head. Why the hesitancy? And why that little hint of unease he could see clouding the edge of her gaze? His presence was obviously making her uncomfortable and Trace couldn't help wondering why.

"Yes. We've been here a few weeks."

"Well, I'm just up the road about four lots, in the white house with the cedar shake roof, if you or your daughter need anything." He smiled at her as he picked up the last shard of glass and set it on her tray.

Definitely a story there, he thought as she hurried away. He just might need to dig a little into her background to find out why someone with fine clothes and nice jewelry, and who so obviously didn't have experience as a waitress, would be here slinging hash at The Gulch. Was she running away from someone? A bad marriage?

So…Rebecca Parsons. Not Becky. An intriguing woman. It had been a long time since one of those had crossed his path here in Pine Gulch.

Trace won't rest until he finds out Rebecca's secret, but will he still have that same attraction to her once he does? Find out in CHRISTMAS IN COLD CREEK. Available November 2011 from Harlequin® Special Edition®.

Harlequin®

ROMANTIC
SUSPENSE

CARLA CASSIDY
Cowboy's Triplet Trouble

Jake Johnson, the eldest of his triplet brothers, is stunned
when Grace Sinclair turns up on his family's ranch declaring
Jake's younger and irresponsible brother as the father of her
triplets. When Grace's life is threatened, Jake finds himself
fighting a powerful attraction and a need to protect. But as
the threats hit closer to home, Jake begins to wonder
if someone on the ranch is out to kill Grace....

A brand-new Top Secret Deliveries story!

TOP SECRET
DELIVERIES

Available in November wherever books are sold!

www.Harlequin.com

HRS27751